LEGENDARY PRIDE

Clint put his beer down. "Who'd start a rumor like that?"

Hartman shrugged. "A woman you slept with who wasn't satisfied?"

Clint gave him a look.

"Okay. A woman you didn't sleep with who wanted to sleep with you?"

"So you don't know who started it?"

"No," Hartman said. "I only know that it came out of Denver."

Clint frowned.

"So I guess you're going to Denver."

"That would be a little shallow, wouldn't it?" Clint asked.

"I guess it would." After a few moments of silence, Hartman said, "When are you leaving?"

"Tomorrow morning."

THE GUNSMITH

181

THE CHALLENGE

J. R. ROBERTS

JOVE BOOKS, NEW YORK

THE CHALLENGE

A Jove Book / published by arrangement with
the author

PRINTING HISTORY
Jove edition / January 1997

The Putnam Berkley World Wide Web site address is
http://www.berkley.com/berkley

ISBN: 0-515-11999-7

A JOVE BOOK®
Jove Books are published by The Berkley Publishing Group,
200 Madison Avenue, New York, New York 10016.
JOVE and the "J" design are trademarks
belonging to Jove Publications, Inc.

PRINTED IN THE UNITED STATES OF AMERICA

10 9 8 7 6 5 4 3 2 1

Prologue

When Darcy Flanders stepped down off the train in Denver she took a deep breath and paused to look around. All of the men in the area, between eight and eighty, paused to watch *her* pause and take a deep breath.

Darcy Flanders was a true beauty. Her red hair cascaded down to her shoulders and back in shimmering waves. Her clothing, while not revealing, clung to her hourglass figure, showing off her hips and breasts to their best advantage.

Her skin was pale, luminous, her eyes large and green. Her nose was straight, her lips full and ripe. She had a long, graceful neck, and beneath her skirt her legs were long and supple, gracefully shaped.

What the men watching her didn't realize was that everything about her was for effect. She knew exactly what she was doing when she did her hair and makeup, and when she chose her clothing. Darcy's intention was to be *extremely* noticeable, and in this she succeeded admirably.

Men hurried to do her bidding even before she asked. One man offered to carry her luggage, another to get her a cab, and still another recommended a hotel. She did not need recommendations, however. She knew exactly what hotel she was going to be staying at. It had all been planned out very carefully.

"The Denver House hotel, please," she told the driver of her horse-drawn cab.

"Yes, ma'am." He would have tried to take her to heaven or hell, if she had asked to go to either.

When she arrived at the hotel, the doorman spotted her right away and raced the driver to help her out of the wagon. As it turned out, they each got to hold one of her hands as she stepped down. The doorman arranged for a bellboy to take her luggage inside, where the desk clerk fell all over himself making sure she got everything she wanted—a room on the third floor, with a bathtub, overlooking the front street.

"Is there anything else I can do for you, Miss Flanders?"

"What's your name, handsome?" she asked.

The desk clerk, who was tall, thin, fifty, and anything but handsome stuck his finger in his collar to loosen it and said, "Ah, Albert, miss."

"Well, Albert, you've been very sweet to me and I appreciate it."

"Think nothing of it, ma'am," Albert said. "Here at the Denver House we try to make our guests as comfortable as possible."

"Well, you're doing a marvelous job. Would you have someone carry my bags to my room, please?"

"But of course," Albert said, snapping his fingers for a bellboy. "That goes without saying."

"And would I be able to get some tea in my room?"

"Right away?"

"Please."

"You'll have it."

"Thank you, Albert." She reached out and cupped his chin in her hand briefly. "You're a sweet man."

Albert opened his mouth to speak, but a squeak came out. He tried to cover it by clearing his throat.

"If you need anything, Miss Flanders," he said, keeping his voice deep, "just ask for it."

"Thank you, I will."

She turned and saw a bellhop in his late forties picking up her bags, tucking them beneath his arms.

"Oh, my," she said, "but you're strong."

He smiled and said, "It's my job, ma'am."

"What's your name?"

"Willie, ma'am."

"Can I help you with one, Willie?"

"No, no, ma'am," the man said, "I have it all. If you'll just take your key—"

"Yes, of course." She turned and accepted the key from Albert, and then followed Willie up the stairs while every man in the lobby—and most of the women—watched.

Over the next three days word got around the hotel that Miss Darcy Flanders was "entertaining" gentlemen in her room. Originally, the employees had wondered if she was, perhaps, a stage actress. She was certainly beautiful enough. Then they wondered if she was just a rich playgirl, here to spend some of her money in Denver.

The last thing they expected to find out was that she was a high-priced prostitute, using her room to entertain her "clients."

This couldn't be tolerated at the Denver House, and it fell to the manager, Pierre Roulet, to tell her this.

Roulet was in his thirties, a fussy man who ran the Denver House like it was his own. He was pear-shaped, with black hair that he slicked down in an attempt to hide its thinness. His mustache was his only conceit. He kept it very carefully trimmed and waxed on the ends.

On the morning of Darcy Flanders's fourth day in the Denver House, Pierre Roulet marched up to her room to tell her that she had to leave. He knocked on the door, and when she answered he was struck dumb by her beauty.

She was wearing a garment he could not describe, except that it showed off her figure without displaying an over-abundance of flesh, and yet it let it be known that there was certainly flesh there—and quite nice flesh it was, too.

"Yes?"

"Miss Flanders, I am Pierre Roulet, the manager of the Denver House."

"Oh, the manager," she said, making her eyes big. "How . . . impressive. You manage the entire hotel?"

"Well . . . yes, I do."

"*All* of its functions come under your supervision?"

"*Oui*, ah, I mean, yes . . ."

"And you are French?" She clapped her hands, de-lighted. "I *love* Frenchmen."

"Ah, yes, really?"

"Please," she said, "I am a bad hostess. Please, come in."

"Uh, yes, thank you," Roulet said—and even as he entered he knew he was thoroughly outclassed.

After the hotel manager left, Darcy sat in front of the mirror in the bedroom and straightened out her hair and her face. When she made her plans for Denver she knew that she would be having sex, both for money, and for free. Mr. Pierre Roulet was one of the free ones. The man's eyes had popped when she had propositioned him, and had almost fallen out when she removed her dressing gown to reveal herself naked beneath it.

"I have heard that Frenchmen are the best lovers, Pierre," she had purred. "Is it true?"

"Mademoiselle . . ." he had said, quickly unbuttoning his shirt and undoing his trousers. . . .

She was surprised that the man was fairly well endowed and also well versed in the art of lovemaking. She watched as he undressed. Although he was stocky, and somewhat soft, he did so without embarrassment.

When she dropped her dressing gown to the floor, he came to her and touched her with his hands, and then his mouth. She was pleasantly surprised to find her body responding to his touch. Since she was having sex with him simply to get her way, she had thought it would be a chore. Very quickly she changed her mind.

"Mmmm," she murmured as he kissed her breasts, sucking her nipples. He held them in his palms gently, as if they were of great value to him, and kissed and sucked them ardently.

When he slipped down between her legs and began to use his tongue there, she would have found it very easy to just lie back and surrender to the sensations she was feeling, but she quickly pushed away the temptation. It had been her intention to show him her skills, not to enjoy his.

"My turn . . ." she said to him, gently turning him onto his back.

His belly was large, but so was his penis, and it was a pretty thing. She slithered down between his legs and took him in both of her hands. She ran her tongue up and down his shaft and then took him fully into her mouth. He moaned as she slid a hand beneath his scrotum to cup his balls and began moving her head, sliding him in and out of her mouth.

As skilled as he obviously was—maybe Frenchmen *were* the best lovers—she was able to take control of the situation eventually and give him more pleasure than he'd ever had before. Apparently no woman had ever been able to do the things that she did with her mouth and her teeth and her fingers, bringing the Frenchman to the brink of completion many times before finally allowing him to finish. All in all it was not an unpleasant experience, except for the fact that his body was rather flabby, and the odor of his perspiration sharp.

After taking Pierre to her bed, she had received his assurance that no one would be back to force her to leave. He would inform the employees that the rumors of her "behavior" were untrue.

"Oh, don't do that," she said.

"Excuse me?"

"Pierre," she said, "darling, I *love* men, and I love having sex. Is that so bad?"

"But . . . no, why should it be?"

"That's what I believe," she said. "I have traveled all over the country, all over the world, in fact, and have had sex with . . . well, *many* men. I've been to bed with princes and kings and . . . well, I've been to bed with Clint Adams."

"Clint Adams?"

"The Gunsmith," she said, her voice almost a whisper.

"Oh, I know who he is," he explained. "He has been a guest here many times."

That gave Darcy some pause, but then she went on bravely.

"Well, he has quite a reputation with the ladies, you know."

"I, uh, did hear something to that effect."

By coincidence she had chosen the same hotel that Clint Adams, the Gunsmith, stayed at when he was in town. She wondered . . .

"Do you know if he, uh, is in Denver . . . now?" she asked.

"Uh, no, not that I know of," Pierre said. "If he was, he would certainly be staying here . . . and I would know."

"I see." She put one hand on his chest "You are *very* important, Pierre."

"I do my job," he said humbly.

She had walked him to the door then and kissed him briefly, causing him to smooth his mustache with the back of his index finger.

"Um . . ." he said, before leaving.

"Yes?"

"If one may ask . . ."

"Of course, Pierre," she said, "anything."

"The Gunsmith . . . well, one wonders how one would measure up against such a man . . . I mean . . ."

She laughed.

"You have nothing to fear, Pierre," she said. "Frenchmen are obviously superior to even American legends."

"Really!" Pierre had said, and he'd left the room very satisfied, and very pleased. Darcy, on the other hand, was unfulfilled. He had excited her with his touch and then she had turned the tables on him, so that she never did achieve her own satisfaction.

She went to the bed, lay down, and touched herself. She had thought to solve the problem that way, but she couldn't concentrate.

Now she was worried about the Gunsmith. They had agreed that she would use his name if the need arose, but only to impress. What if he appeared in Denver while she was there? That would be a catastrophic coincidence.

She was going to have to have something done to make sure that didn't happen.

ONE

Rick Hartman sat behind his desk, holding a brandy snifter between his hands, using his own body heat to warm the wonderful liquid while he pondered his predicament.

He was sitting in his office in his Labyrinth, Texas, saloon called Rick's Place. His predicament was this: he had recently heard rumors about his friend, Clint Adams, and he was trying to decide if he should tell him about it. The reason he was unsure was that the rumors did not concern Clint personally—that is, they were not attacks on his reputation. At least, not his reputation as the Gunsmith, per se . . . it was even confusing to Hartman to think about it and try to reason it out.

The rumors had to do with his friend's sexual prowess, and they were certainly not rumors that were circulating in general circles. He was getting his information from a knowledgeable source in Denver that there was a woman staying at the Denver House—an establishment he knew for a fact Clint frequented when in Denver—who was claiming to have slept with him and not been impressed. However, this woman was apparently sleeping with a lot of men in Denver, which made Hartman curious. After all, the Denver House was hardly a bordello.

The trouble, though, was whether or not to tell Clint of the rumors. There was always a chance he'd never hear them, but then the opposite was also true. If Clint was going to hear the rumors, then Hartman thought it should come from a friend. Since he currently considered himself to be Clint's best friend—rivaled, perhaps, by the likes of Bat Masterson—he decided he would be the one.

He was waiting now for Clint to arrive for lunch, a date they had made the day before. Clint had already made it known that he was leaving Labyrinth tomorrow, a trip with an indistinct destination.

Hartman didn't think he could predict whether or not his information would make Clint Adams's destination clearer.

Clint rolled over and glanced at the light coming in the window. It was afternoon, and he had a lunch appointment with Rick Hartman. He turned his head and looked at the girl lying in bed next to him. She was lying with her back to him, her knees drawn up to her belly. He looked at the light again, guessing how much time he had before he was supposed to meet Rick. Figuring that he had just enough time, he rolled over and pressed himself against the girl's naked butt. She moaned and pressed back against him, even though she was still half asleep. His penis swelled and he rubbed it against the cleft between her ass cheeks. She straightened her legs and spread her thighs so that he was able to slide his erection between them. He was surprised at how wet she was already, and he slid into her with ease. He began to move in and out of her, and she sighed and reached around behind them to rub her hand over his ass.

"I thought you were going to have lunch with Rick?" she asked.

"I am," he said, "but first I've got to work up an appetite. Do you think you can help me do that?"

She did something that caused her insides to tighten around him.

"I think I can handle that."

Clint walked into Rick's Place a half an hour late for lunch. There wasn't much business at that time of day.

"Where is he?" he asked the bartender.

"In his office, havin' lunch."

"Thanks," Clint said. "I'll take a beer in with me."

The bartender drew it and handed it over, and Clint went to the office door and knocked.

"Come."

He entered and saw Hartman sitting at a table set up in the middle of the office.

"Sit down," Hartman said around a mouthful of food. "I decided not to wait for you."

Clint pulled out a chair and sat opposite Hartman. He sipped his beer and put it down, noticing that his friend was having some of that fine brandy he liked.

"Sorry I'm late."

"You took Lisa home last night, didn't you?"

"Uh-huh."

"Well, that explains it," Hartman said. "Looks like she won her bet."

"Bet?" Clint asked. "What bet?"

"She had a bet with the other girls—you know, some of whom you've also slept with—that she could keep you in bed past noon."

Clint frowned.

"Well, then," he said, "I guess she did win her bet, didn't she."

Hartman stopped chewing his food and picked up his brandy.

"Are you offended?"

Clint thought a minute.

"I don't know," he said finally. "I did enjoy the night, and the morning . . ."

"And the afternoon?"

"Yes."

"So then why be offended?"

"I don't know," Clint said. "Maybe I should feel like a piece of meat."

"If that offends you," Hartman said, "I've got something that you're really not going to like."

"What's that?"

"Maybe I should wait until after lunch."

Clint looked down at his plate, which had some sort of glazed chicken on it. Hartman had recently begun eating more fancy foods, while Clint continued to enjoy simpler fare, like stews and steaks.

"Why don't we talk during lunch? What is this on the chicken?"

"Some kind of apricot glaze."

"Apricot? What is that?"

"It's a fruit."

"Not one I ever heard of."

He poked it.

"Well, it's dead, so I'll eat it."

"What's wrong with trying to improve my palate?"

"Your what?"

"Palate," Hartman said.

Clint cut a piece and put it in his mouth.

"Well?"

"Rather have a steak," Clint said. "What did you want to tell me?"

"Well . . ."

"Spit it out, Rick."

"There are some rumors going around about you."

"What else is new?"

"Well, I'm talking about one rumor in particular."

"Which one is that?"

"Um, it's about your, uh, prowess . . ."

"Which prowess is that?"

"In the, uh, bedroom."

Clint stopped eating.

"Where?"

"The—"

"I heard you. Are you serious?"

"Yes."

"That's ridiculous."

They ate in silence for a few moments, and then Clint put down his fork and picked up his beer.

"All right," Clint said, "tell me. Where did this rumor originate?"

"Denver."

"Denver? I haven't been to Denver for months."

"Well, apparently there's a woman staying at the Denver House who claims to have slept with you."

"When?"

"That I don't know."

"What's her name?"

"I don't know that either."

"Well, then, what's the rumor?"

"Well . . . apparently she said you weren't very good."

Clint sipped his beer and stared at his friend. "Are you making this up?"

"No," Hartman said. "Why would I?"

Clint put his beer down. "Who'd start a rumor like that?"

Hartman shrugged. "A woman you slept with who wasn't satisfied?"

Clint gave him a look.

"Okay, a woman you didn't sleep with who wanted to sleep with you?"

"So you don't know who started it?"

"No," Hartman said. "I only know that it came out of Denver."

Clint frowned.

"So I guess you're going to Denver?"

"That would be a little shallow, wouldn't it?" Clint asked. "Going all the way to Denver because someone criticized my performance in bed?"

"I guess it would." After a few moments of silence Hartman said, "When are you leaving?"

"Tomorrow morning."

TWO

Darcy Flanders had been in Denver a week now, spending most of her time in her room, entertaining. On this day, however, she left her room early in the morning and went down to the lobby of the hotel. The manager, Pierre Roulet, was behind the desk and she graced him with a smile. The young desk clerk, Jefferson, standing next to Roulet, observed the exchange and was even more certain now that the lady had given her favors to Roulet in return for not being booted out of the hotel. He greatly looked forward to the day when he would be a hotel manager and be eligible for such favors.

Darcy left the hotel, turned left, and walked three blocks until she came to a restaurant called Luigi's. She had acquired a taste for Italian food while living and working in the East, and upon arrival in Denver had sought out and found this restaurant. She had not eaten there as yet, preferring to save the place for meetings like this one.

She entered and gave her name to the maître d', who bowed, said how wonderful it was to have such a lovely lady grace their establishment, and then showed her to a very private table in a corner. She ordered wine and said she would wait for her "gentleman friend" to arrive before ordering.

"He is a cad," the maître d' said, "if he keeps you waiting even one second longer."

"What is your name, please?" she asked.

"Ah, I am Carlo, madam."

"Carlo," she said, saying the name in such a way as to send shivers down the man's spine, "I am sure I am going to like this place."

"I will have your waiter bring your wine immediately!"

"Thank you, Carlo."

She had just received her wine from an admiring waiter when a man entered and spoke to the maître d', Carlo, who gave him a stern look and showed him to Darcy's table.

"What's wrong with him?" the man asked.

"He doesn't think you should have kept a delicate flower like me waiting."

"Delicate flower?" the man repeated. "What would he say if he knew that you could kill him with one hand?"

"I think he would say that he'd die happy."

She looked across the table at her partner, John Cable. He was in his early thirties and was possibly the handsomest man she had ever seen. She and Cable had been working together for five years now, and although she'd been to bed with many men during that time—for both business and pleasure—they had never been to bed together.

"The minute we're not partners anymore," she had said to him once, "I'll race you to the nearest bed."

So far, however, their partnership was still too valuable to them to risk it, or end it.

"So, how's it going?" he asked. Then he quickly added, "Where's the waiter? I'm hungry."

"Never mind you're hungry," she said, leaning forward, her tone becoming less ladylike, "somebody's made a mess of things already."

"What do you mean?"

"Clint Adams!" she said. "Whose bright idea was it for us to use his name?"

"You know whose idea it was," Cable said. "Do you want to criticize *him*?"

"I would," she said, "you wouldn't. He's your hero, not mine."

"So what's the problem?"

"The problem is that when Adams is in Denver he stays at the Denver House hotel."

"Uh-oh," Cable said, "that could be a problem—but then, it would be a coincidence if he came to town just now, wouldn't it?"

"And how many of those have we run into over the years?" she asked facetiously.

"Okay, okay, so it was a bad idea," Cable admitted, "but we're stuck with it now, unless you want to pull out."

"I'm not pulling out," Darcy said. "I want this guy."

"Do you still think this plan is gonna work?" Cable asked.

"It'll work," she said. "You can always count on a man's ego, John."

"Oh, really?"

"Sure," she said, "tweak a man's ego, especially about his manhood, and he becomes very predictable."

"Is that so?"

"Are you getting insulted for all men?" she asked.

"No," he said, "not all men."

"Poor John," she said, reaching out and touching his hand. "You know none of my generalizations about the male sex include you, don't you? You're special."

He stared at her for a few moments, then slid his hand

from beneath hers and said, "You sure can shovel it with the best of them, Darcy. Now, where is that waiter?"

Darcy withdrew her hand. She did think he was special, and different, but it was just as well he didn't take her seriously.

After lunch they sat and had an after-dinner drink, discussing their plan further.

"I've been able to watch your window," he said, "from across the way."

"How did you get into that building?"

"Let's just say no one knows I'm there. If you need me just open and close the curtain twice and I'll be there in minutes."

"All right."

"How have you been doing with the men?"

"I'm about twenty dollars ahead."

Most of the men who had been coming to her room as "johns" actually worked for the same people Darcy and Cable did, and they whiled away the time playing straight-up poker, while people assumed they were having sex. So far, she'd only had to deliver once, and that was with the hotel manager, and that had not been an unpleasant experience at all. It hadn't been fulfilling for her, but certainly not unpleasant.

"I get half of that, right?"

"Right."

"Well, keep strict accounts."

They finished their drinks and sat there awkwardly. Darcy had no way of knowing how upsetting it was to Cable when she had to use sex in their work. Cable had no way of knowing how little that kind of sex meant to Darcy. All sex might have meant nothing to her, since her virginity had been taken by a father and two brothers when she was eleven, but she had managed to overcome that handicap and now enjoyed sex very much—usually on her own terms.

She often wondered, though, how sex would be with a man she truly liked, and admired and respected and . . . maybe even loved.

How would it be, for instance, with Cable?

"Well," she said, "I have to get back."

"Darcy . . ."

"Yes?"

She realized then and there that if he asked her to abandon their plan, she would.

"How long are we going to go on with this?"

"Until he comes out of the woodwork, Cable," she said, "and we catch him."

"There's a lot of money being spent here."

She smiled and said, "Our employers can afford it, can't they?"

"I guess they can."

"Okay . . ." she said, waiting to see if he had anything else to say. "I'll be getting back."

"We meet here again in three days if nothing happens?" he asked.

"Right."

"If you need to see me before then," he said, "let one of your poker buddies know, and they'll pass the message on to me."

"Okay."

"Oh, yeah," he said, "there's a bellboy named Wilson. He's new in the hotel. He's with us. If need be, you can use him for messages."

"Got it."

"Be careful, Darcy," he said as she stood up. "Lyle Jason has killed a lot of people."

"I know," she said, "that's exactly why we're trying to take him out of circulation, isn't it?"

Cable watched as Darcy left, taking the eyes of every man and woman in the place with her, and then signaled for the waiter so he could pay the bill.

THREE

Lyle Jason looked down at the whore who was on her knees in front of him. His penis was raging, and she was holding it in her hands like it was something sacred.

"You gonna suck it," he asked, "or pray to it?"

The whore looked up at him, her eyes unsure and frightened. She knew from talking to the other girls that if she didn't do something special, something fabulous, she might not get away without a few bruises. She also knew that when Jason did bruise girls, he usually paid them a little more to make up for it. There were those times, though, when he actually hurt girls so much that a few extra dollars didn't make up for it.

Valerie Burke didn't use her real name when she was

working. Her whore name was "Empress." She thought it sounded regal.

Jason had been to Mona's Whorehouse, in Little Fork, New Mexico, at least six other times, and he'd taken a different girl each time. Empress was the seventh, and she was hoping that the seventh time was the charm.

She knew that she had made grown men beg by sucking their dicks, and she hoped to use all of her talents to satisfy Lyle Jason, who—it was said—was a connoisseur of whores.

She gripped his large penis in one fist and lowered her mouth over it. She heard him growl and felt his hands on her head, but as she was about to begin sucking in earnest there was a knock at the door.

"What?" Jason shouted.

"Lyle, it's me."

"Come on in, damn it." He looked down at Empress and asked, "Why are you stopping? Keep suckin'."

The door opened and Jason's partner, Earl Terry, walked in.

Terry was Jason's age—thirty-four—but there the similarities ended. While Jason was a slender man standing under six feet, Terry was a hulking brute of a man, towering at about six eight. He entered and saw the girl on her knees, sucking his partner's cock. It was a sight he had seen many times before. He was almost as familiar with the sight of Jason's penis as he was with his own, and the fact that Jason's was larger than his was of no concern to him whatsoever. In fact, sex was of nearly no concern to him at all, and when he did crave it he chose to get it over with as soon as possible—not that he enjoyed it, but so that the craving would stop.

The girl's head began bobbing up and down, and Jason began moving his hips, fucking her mouth.

"Well?" Jason asked.

"The word from Denver is that this lady has taken a

room at the Denver House hotel. She's supposed to be a very high-class whore, very particular about her clients."

"Is that a fact?"

Terry didn't know how Jason could concentrate on what they were saying while the girl was sucking on him. She was making wet noises now, which Terry found not only distracting, but distasteful.

"It is," Terry said. "She's supposed to be the best, Lyle."

"And who is starting these rumors?" Jason asked. "Her?"

"I don't know."

"Well, I guess there's one way to find out," Jason said. "Okay, that's enough."

He was speaking to the whore. He grabbed her head by the hair and pulled her off his cock, then slapped her in the face. The blow sent her sprawling.

"You're the worst cocksucker of the bunch," he said. "Tell Mona to send up Princess. She's the only one who ever got me to finish."

"O-okay—" Empress said, starting to crawl toward the door.

"Wait a minute."

The naked Jason put his foot on the girl's back and pushed her flat to the floor, holding her that way.

"You want this one?" he asked Terry.

His partner scowled and said, "No."

"Okay," Jason said, taking his foot off the small of the girl's back, "get out!"

She got back to her hands and knees and scurried for the door, but didn't make it in time to avoid a well-placed kick to her buttocks.

"Why do you treat them like that?" Terry asked.

"Because they were born to be treated like that," Jason said. "They're whores, Earl."

"Yeah. What about this Denver one?"

"What's her name?"

Terry frowned, then dredged it up from his memory.

"Darcy."

"That her real name?"

"Far as I know."

"No whore name, huh? That's interesting."

"Interesting enough to go to Denver?"

"Yeah," Jason said, absently stroking his distended prick while he thought, "yeah, I think so."

Terry stood up and said, "I'll leave you alone then, and you can finish. I'll wait outside."

As Terry left the room Jason became aware of the fact that he was stroking himself. He looked down at his hand and the huge, pink penis in it, and then there was a light knock on the door and Princess entered. She was Oriental, with long black hair and a little cupid's bow mouth, and of the seven whores he'd had here at Mona's she was the only one who had left this room unbruised.

"Ah, there you are," he said, pulling harder on his cock, "bring that sweet little mouth over here, Princess. I got something for you."

Princess smiled and didn't even bother to remove her filmy dressing gown. She got down on her knees and took Jason's penis into her mouth. She just had to remember what she had done last time to make him happy. . . .

"That's it, you dirty little whore," he said as she sucked on him. "I'm leavin' town tomorrow. Gimme somethin' to remember you by. . . ."

Earl Terry found a chair outside the whorehouse and sat down in it. They'd been in New Mexico too long and he was looking forward to leaving. He'd never been to Denver and he thought that while Lyle Jason was busy with his whoring, he could take a look around the big city. He was a big man and tired of small towns. Maybe a big city like Denver was just the place for him. Maybe after Denver he'd go to even bigger cities, like San Francisco, or Chicago, or

New York. There should be plenty of whores in those places for Lyle Jason, and Terry had never once considered going anywhere without Jason, so why should this be any different?

FOUR

When Clint walked into the lobby of the Denver House he paused a moment, as if to say "I'm here," and let everyone see. When nothing happened he realized how silly he was being and walked up to the desk.

"Can I help you, sir?" the clerk asked.

"Yes, I'd like a room."

"Do you have a reservation?"

"No," Clint said, "but I'm hoping you can find a room for me."

"Well, we are quite full—"

"I always stay here when I'm in Denver," Clint said. "You've always been able to accommodate me in the past."

"Well, er, sir, what is your name?"

"Adams," Clint said, "Clint Adams."

The clerk, who had been looking down at his reservation book, jerked his head up and stared right at Clint.

"Mr. Adams?"

"That's right."

"Clint Adams?"

"Still right," Clint said. "Can you help me out?"

"Ah, I believe I can, sir," the clerk said. "Just give me a moment?"

"Sure," Clint said, "take all the time you need . . . as long as you come back and tell me you can give me a room."

The clerk went through a doorway behind the desk and hurried to the manager's office. He entered without knocking.

Pierre Roulet looked up from his desk with a scowl on his face.

"What is it, Jefferson? Have you forgotten how to knock?"

"Mr. Roulet," Jefferson said, "there's a guest at the front desk I think you will be interested in."

"And who might that be, Jefferson?" Roulet asked, looking back down at his desk.

"Uh, Clint Adams, sir."

Roulet's head jerked up.

"Adams?"

"Yes, sir."

"Clint Adams?"

"That's right, sir."

Roulet thought a moment.

"Does he have a reservation?"

"No, sir, but, he—uh, he's insistent that we are always able to accommodate him."

"Well . . . of course we are. He is an old and valued guest."

"B-but, Mr. Roulet—"

"Give him a room, Jefferson."

"Sir?"

"A good room, on the second floor."

"The second floor," Jefferson said, "yes, sir."

"We're always able to take care of Mr. Adams," Roulet said. "Make sure he knows that."

"Yes, sir."

"Go now!"

Jefferson turned and went back outside to register Clint Adams as a guest in the hotel.

After Jefferson left, Roulet got up from his desk and went out the door of his office. Instead of making a left as Jefferson had done, he made a right and walked to the back of the hotel. There he made his way up the back stairs to the third floor and hurried to Darcy Flanders's door. He knocked hurriedly, hoping that she was inside. He'd been in his office all morning and she could have left without him seeing her. Damn it, he should have asked Jefferson about that.

He knocked again, this time with his palm.

FIVE

"Pair of aces," Darcy said. "You lose again."

Shane Mack threw his cards down. They flipped and revealed that he'd had a pair of kings.

"Darcy, if I didn't know you better I'd swear you were cheating."

Darcy laughed, because Mack *didn't* know her well, and she was cheating him. She had learned how to bottom deal years ago, and while she'd never try it on a professional, Mack couldn't tell which part of the deck the cards were coming from.

"I'm just lucky, Mack," she said, gathering up the cards for her deal.

Before she could deal, someone started knocking on the door insistently.

"Who could that be?" she wondered aloud.

"An anxious customer?" Mack asked.

"You're my customer for this hour, Mack."

"Oh, yeah."

The knocking continued, the tone changing, as if who-ever it was had stopped using his knuckles and was using his palm.

"Get behind the door," Darcy said, and they both got up from the table.

Mack flattened himself against the wall behind the door, his gun in his hand, and Darcy opened.

"Mr. Roulet," she said. "How nice, but . . . I *am* a little busy at the moment."

"Something has happened . . . Miss Flanders . . . that you should know about."

"And what might that be, Mr. Roulet?"

The manager was out of breath from his run up the stairs and his frantic beating on her door.

"Clint . . . Adams . . ."

"Catch your breath, Mr. Roulet," Darcy said. "What about Clint Adams?"

"He's . . . here."

"Here?" she repeated. "At the hotel?"

He nodded, his red face slowly returning to its true color.

"Has he registered?"

"Yes."

"Did you have to give him a room?"

Roulet looked shocked.

"Yes."

Darcy knew that if he had told her about it before Adams registered and she had let him fuck her, he would have refused to give Adams a room, but it was too late now. Besides, she didn't want to let this fussy little man have her again.

"What floor did you give him a room on?"

"Two."

"All right," she said. "Thank you, Mr. Roulet—al-though I don't know why you feel you had to warn me."

"I was just . . . giving you some information, Miss Flanders."

"Of course," she said. "Thank you."

He executed a small bow and she closed the door. Mack holstered his gun.

"He must know that you lied about Adams."

"It doesn't matter what he thinks," she said. "He's harmless. It's Adams I'm worried about. What's he *doing* here?"

"Coincidence?"

"Maybe," she said, "but if he hasn't heard what I've said about him, he'll have to hear it now that he's here."

"Why?"

"Because men like to gossip, Mack."

"What? Women like to gossip, Darcy."

She gave him a look.

"What are you talking about? Men are the biggest gossips ever."

"Oh, please—"

"If you heard that a woman you know had slept with Cable and said he wasn't very good—or, better yet, if she'd slept with both of you and said that you were better, what would you do?"

"Well, I'd, uh . . ."

"You'd tell him, wouldn't you?"

"I would not."

"Well, you'd tell somebody, wouldn't you?"

"Well . . ."

"Sure, you would," she said. "You'd have to, or bust." He frowned at her.

"Okay, you won't admit it, but you know it. Get out of here."

He grabbed his jacket and said, "Do what?"

"Go and tell Cable that Clint Adams is here."

"And then what?"

"And then you geniuses will have to figure out a way to make sure he never sees me."

"What do you want us to do?" he asked. "Make him leave town by sundown?"

He laughed, and then noticed that she wasn't joining in. "Darcy?"

"That's not a bad idea, Mack."

"Hey, I was just kidd—"

"Well, I'm not," she said. "Go and tell Cable you need a plan."

"But, Darc—"

"Now!"

SIX

After Mack left the room, Darcy walked to the window and looked outside. She remembered what Cable had told her about using the curtain to signal him, but the last thing she wanted right now was him rushing over. Let Mack explain things to him.

She turned and walked to the armchair in the room and sat down. She started to gnaw a nail, caught herself, and placed her hands in her lap. This job was risky right from the beginning, when she first thought of it, but the suggestion to use Clint Adams's name made it even more risky. Why had she agreed to that? What were the chances, others had asked, of actually running into him on this job?

How about a hundred out of a hundred?

• • •

Clint entered his room and put his gear down next to the bed. It was stupid to come all this way because someone had slighted his sexual prowess, but he'd always maintained that he was just a man, and nothing special. They called him the Gunsmith, but he knew he was mostly just like anyone else, and now he was proving it by coming all this way to find a woman who claimed to have been to bed with him. Like any other man, maybe his ego was a bit bruised by the rumors.

Well, at the very least, while he was here he could stop in and see his friend, Talbot Roper. Roper was probably the best private detective in the business, and although his work took him all over the country, and the world, he made his home base Denver. He only hoped that Roper was in town and not away on some case.

He walked to the window and looked out. People were walking by; a man was rushing across the street as if someone was chasing him. Clint wasn't sure what his first move should be. How did he find a woman whose name he didn't know, whom he'd never seen? Well, since he was going to see his friend Roper anyway, he might as well present the problem to him and see what he had to suggest.

He decided to leave the room and go to see Roper now. Better to get started right away than waste time.

Shane Mack hurried across the street, then made his way around to the back of the building that was directly opposite the Denver House hotel. He found the door that Cable had forced when he first got into the building and entered. He made his way up the stairs to the third floor, and then down a hall to a door. He knocked twice, then knocked once and entered.

Cable turned from the window and asked, "What are you doing here?" He had the remains of a sandwich on the floor next to him, and a pot of coffee. There was no furniture in the room.

"Bet you're real comfortable here," Mack said.

"I asked you what you're doing here, Shane," Cable repeated.

"Darcy sent me."

"Why? What's wrong?"

"Clint Adams."

"What about him?"

Mack leaned over and peered out the window.

"Which window is hers?"

"What about Adams, Mack?" Cable asked.

Cable and Mack were not the best of friends. Each thought they were superior to the other, and Mack couldn't understand why Cable got to partner with Darcy, and not him. He was jealous of Cable, assuming that he and Darcy were lovers as well as partners.

"He's here."

"In Denver?"

"At this hotel."

"Jesus!" Cable said. "What the hell is he doing here?"

Mack shrugged and said, "I don't know," even though the question wasn't really directed at him.

"We're going to have to take care of this," Cable said.

"Tell me, Cable," Mack said, "how do you 'take care' of a living legend?"

"We'll figure it out," Cable said. "Right now you've got to stay here."

"Why?"

"Because I've got to tell the others about this—"

"I can do that."

"—and send a telegram to Washington."

Mack couldn't do that, because he wasn't in charge.

"Okay."

Cable stood up and pulled on his jacket, which would cover the gun he was wearing under his left arm in a shoulder rig.

"I'll be back as soon as I can."

"Yeah, sure."

Mack had done this kind of duty before. Usually everybody forgot about you.

Cable headed for the door and Mack sat on the floor by the window. He looked at Cable's half-eaten sandwich, wondering what kind it was. He waited until the other man left, and then picked it up and smelled it. His stomach growled, and he took a bite.

Cable was upset. If Clint Adams heard anything about Darcy and confronted her, he could ruin the whole deal. There had to be some way to handle him, living legend or not.

SEVEN

Clint entered Roper's office and saw that, once again, the man had a different secretary than the last time he'd been there. This one was not as young as some of the others, and had more poise. Her appearance was stern, but Clint could see that she was attractive beneath it.

"Can I help you?" she asked.

"I'd like to see Mr. Roper."

"Do you have an appointment?"

"No, but I think he'll see me. I'm an old friend."

"And you are . . . ?"

"Clint Adams."

Her demeanor changed immediately.

"Oh, yes, Mr. Adams! Of course. Mr. Roper has told me about you."

"He has?"

"Yes, sir."

"How much?"

With just the hint of a smile she said, "Just that you were friends, and that if you ever walked in I was to let him know immediately."

Just from that small smile Clint knew that Talbot Roper had told her more than that.

"If you'll wait just a moment, I'll let him know that you're here."

"Thank you."

She went into Roper's office, closing the door behind her, then came out moments later and held it open for him.

"Mr. Roper will see you now."

"Thank you . . ."

"Pearl."

"Ah, thank you, Pearl."

He went inside and she closed the door behind her.

"Pearl?" Clint said to Roper, who was seated behind his desk.

He stood up, a tall, well-built man about Clint's age, and extended his hand.

"And isn't she one?" Roper asked. "How are you, Clint?"

"I'm good, Tal."

The two men shook hands warmly.

"Brandy?" Roper asked.

"Uh, I'd rather get out of here and buy you a beer," Clint said. "I have something, um, delicate to talk to you about."

"All right," Roper said. "We'll go down the street to Bailey's."

"New place?"

"Opened since the last time you were here. Good Irish food, good beer, great Irish whiskey."

Roper came around the desk, grabbing his jacket from behind his chair and pulling it on. He slapped Clint on the back and opened the door.

"Pearl, we'll be at Bailey's for lunch."

"This early?"

"Pearl," Roper said, "I'm the boss, I can go to lunch whenever I like."

"Yes, sir, Mr. Roper."

"Good-bye, Pearl."

"It was a pleasure to meet you, Mr. Adams."

"Come on, come on, out," Roper said, pushing Clint.

"What's the rush?" Clint asked outside.

"She's your type," Roper said. "I don't want you charming her, she'll be lost to me for days. Now, what's this problem you have?"

"Well, it's not exactly a problem, it's more like . . ."

"A dilemma?"

"Exactly."

"Well, spit it out, boy," Roper said, "I'm a whiz with dilemmas."

"I think I'll wait until we each have a beer in front of us."

"Well, let's step up the pace, then. It's just another block."

EIGHT

Bailey's was a small but plush place, all green and mahogany, with gray-haired waiters in vests and bow ties who waited quietly until the customer was ready to order. Roper and Clint were shown to a corner table Clint assumed was Roper's regular spot.

"Two beers, Michael," Roper said to the waiter.

"Comin' up, sir." The waiter had just the hint of an Irish accent.

"Sometimes I wish I'd been born Irish," Roper said.

"Why?"

"Well, for one thing," he said, "the women are lovely, and they seem to prefer their Irish men."

"That sounds like a good enough reason."

The waiter returned with two beers.

"Thank you, Michael."

They waited until the waiter was out of earshot.

"All right," Roper said, "you've kept me waiting long enough. What's this dilemma of yours?"

"It's . . . going to sound silly."

"Try me."

Clint told him the story of the rumor, and Roper listened intently until he was done . . . and then laughed.

"I'm sorry," he said, "but it does sound funny."

"And what would you think if the rumor was about you?" Clint asked.

Roper frowned.

"Well, then I guess it wouldn't be so funny."

"Thank you."

"But you've never before struck me as a man with something to prove, uh, in that area."

"I don't think it's the subject of the rumor that brought me here," Clint said, "so much as the fact that there *was* a rumor."

"And you want to find out who's spreading it?"

"Yes."

"Besides the woman, that is."

"I'd like to know who she is, too," Clint said. "I'd like to find out if I know her."

"Well, I think I can solve half your problem."

"You can? Already?"

"Well, the word got around pretty quickly about this woman at the Denver House. Very high-class, very beautiful, and very busy."

"As a whore, you mean?"

Roper nodded.

"Why would the Denver House allow a woman like that to stay there?"

"The manager is a man."

"Just like that? He's getting a sample, so he's letting her stay?"

"That's what I heard."

"What else did you hear?" Clint asked. "Did you happen to hear the woman's name?"

"Darcy Flanders."

"Darcy Flanders," Clint repeated, then said it several times again below his breath.

"Do you know her?" Roper asked.

"I don't think I do," Clint said, then added, "not under that name, anyway. What does she look like?"

"I haven't seen her," Roper said. "All I know is what I told you."

"I'll have to see her for myself, then."

"Maybe you know her under another name."

"Maybe."

"What do you plan to do?"

"What can I do, but talk to her."

"Well . . . you could try to prove the rumor wrong."

"That's not what I'm here for, Tal."

"It was just a thought."

"Are you going to be in town for a while?"

"I've got nowhere to go," Roper said. "Business is slow, for a change."

"Good," Clint said, "maybe we can have dinner before I leave."

"Sure, I'd like that."

"Maybe you could bring Pearl along?"

"Maybe not," Roper said.

"How long do you think you'll keep this secretary, Tal?" Clint asked.

"A lot longer if I keep her away from you," Roper said. "You want another beer?"

NINE

Lyle Jason and Earl Terry arrived in Denver a few hours after Clint Adams, on the same day. They did not have the money to stay in the Denver House hotel, however, so they stayed in a place some distance from there, in an entirely different neighborhood. They also didn't have enough money to get separate rooms, so they were sharing one, with two beds.

"We've got to find a way to make some money while we're here, Lyle," Terry said, reclining on his bed with his hands behind his neck.

Jason was sitting on his bed, facing Terry.

"We've never had any trouble doing that before, have we, boy?" he asked. "Making money's the one thing we know how to do."

41

"This is different, Lyle," Terry said. "This is Denver, a big city."

"Have you ever been to a big city before, Earl?"

"No."

"Well, you're in luck, boy," Jason said. "I'm gonna show it to you."

"You been here before?" Terry asked.

"Sure I have."

"You ever been to any other big cities?"

"A few."

"Like what?"

"St. Louis."

"That's a big city?"

"Sure it is."

"What else?"

"A few."

"Have you even been to New York?"

"No."

"San Francisco?"

"No."

"I'd like to go to those places."

"So would I, but why don't we start with Denver?"

"What are we gonna do here, Lyle? You just want to find that girl."

"Yeah, I do, but while I'm doing that we can also take a look at the city. It's not like a town, you know, it's real different."

"It's big," Terry said.

As big as Earl Terry was, he had felt small during the ride from the train station to the hotel. This was *nothing* like being in a small Western town, and he wasn't sure he was going to like it—but he had to find out for sure. If he didn't like it here, there wouldn't be any point in going to New York or San Francisco.

"Whataya say?" Jason asked. "You want to go out and take a look around?"

"What about . . ."

"What about what?"

"Well . . . you're wanted in lots of places, Lyle."

"Not in Denver," Jason said. "Come on, whataya say?"

"Sure," Terry said, "why not."

"Let's go, then," Jason said. "It's time for you to get a taste of the city."

TEN

There were three men working with John Cable and Darcy Flanders other than Shane Mack. One was Ron Wilson, who was working in the hotel as a bellboy to be close to her. The other two were Dave Selby and Will Blake. The three of them and Cable were now in a room in a hotel a block from the Denver House that they were using for meetings.

"What's going on?" Blake asked.

"Do you know?" Cable asked Wilson.

"I know Clint Adams checked into the hotel today," Wilson said. "Is that why we're here?"

"What?" Selby asked.

"That's why we're here," Cable said. "What can we do about it?"

"Why do we have to do anything?" Blake asked.

"Darcy used Adams's name to make herself more visible, and to build herself up," Cable explained. "If he heard about it and went looking for her, he could cause us some trouble."

"So what are we supposed to do about it?" Blake asked.

Cable frowned, because he'd just asked the same question.

"You want us to take Adams out?" Selby asked.

Cable knew that Selby was asking if he wanted Adams killed.

"No," he said, "there's no reason to kill him. Maybe we can come up with a way to distract him."

"And how could we do that?"

"Well, he's got several reputations," Cable said, "one of which is with the ladies."

"Well," Selby said, "Darcy's done that some damage, hasn't she?"

"Whose bright idea was it to use his name?" Blake asked.

"Never mind," Cable said, wanting to avoid answering that question. He was the one who had done the research on Clint Adams. He knew how dangerous the man was. He wondered—as everyone else was now—what had possessed him to choose Clint Adams's name to use in building up Darcy's reputation.

"What's the other reputation for?" Blake asked.

"Trouble."

"We can cause him some of that," Selby said.

"Nothing dangerous, remember," Cable said, "just a distraction."

"When do we need this by?" Wilson asked.

"As soon as possible," Cable said. "If he hears the rumor about Darcy, we don't want him to go looking for her, do we?"

Selby and Blake exchanged a glance. They had worked together before, and each had worked with Cable before. Wilson was new to the group.

"So we do what?" Wilson asked. "Meet back here tomorrow?"

"In the morning," Cable said, "and somebody better have an idea."

"Does that include you?" Blake asked.

"Yes, it includes me."

Of course, Cable thought, as the others filed out, it was his last big idea that had gotten them into this mess, wasn't it?

ELEVEN

Clint returned to the Denver House and stopped at the desk.

"Yes, sir?" the young clerk asked.

"Do you have a Darcy Flanders registered?"

"Uh, Darcy—uh, Fland—I'll have to check—uh—" the clerk stammered.

"I'll make it easier for you," Clint said. "I know she's registered. All you have to tell me is what room she's in."

"Well, sir, we, uh, don't give out the, uh, room numbers of our guests, uh, usually—"

"Who can I get it from?"

"Well, you'd have to talk to the manager."

"And what's his name?"

"Mr. Roulet."

"And is he in now?"

"Uh, not at the moment, sir."

"And will he be in?"

"I'm not sure, sir, but I can, uh, check—"

"I tell you what," Clint said. "When he does come in you tell him that Mr. Adams in room 212 wants to talk to him. All right?"

"Uh, yes, sir, I'll do that," the clerk said, "as soon as he comes in."

"Thanks."

Clint's other option was to sit in the lobby and wait to see if Darcy Flanders came down. He felt sure he'd know her on sight—that is, from the amount of attention she drew he'd know who she was. He doubted that he was going to know her by sight—or that he had ever met her before. He didn't know any woman who would claim to have known him and been to bed with him, then denigrate his performance, all to enhance her own reputation as a high-priced whore. He just couldn't believe that kind of woman would have ever appealed to him.

He decided to go into the hotel bar, have a drink, and see if he could get to the hotel manager today. If not, then maybe he'd just start pounding on doors in the morning.

John Cable was already in the hotel bar when Clint Adams entered. He watched as Adams went to the bar, got a beer, and then carried it to a back table. He'd thought it best to keep an eye on Adams. If the man had any thoughts of finding Darcy and talking to her tonight, he figured he might be able to head him off. At the moment, however, the man seemed content to sit and sip his beer.

When Clint was seated at a back table with a beer, he admitted to himself that knocking on doors was not an option. He did, however, decide that Darcy Flanders would probably have one of the better rooms in the hotel. It probably wouldn't be hard to find out some choice room numbers and then check them out. A few dollars to a willing bellboy would take care of that.

He thought again of how silly this entire trip probably was. He probably should just forget about the whole thing, continue on to California, and have a good time. Still, his curiosity needed to be satisfied as to who this woman was.

Clint looked around the room, which was half full. Through another doorway he could see the dining room. He wondered if this Darcy Flanders took her meals down here, or in her room. Thinking about meals made him realize that he was hungry. He finished off his beer, got up, and walked to the dining room.

Cable wondered if he should take a chance of being spotted by following Adams into the dining room. What could the man be doing in there but having a meal? Or maybe he was expecting to see Darcy eating in there?

Cable decided to leave Adams alone for the moment and take the opportunity to go upstairs and talk to Darcy.

TWELVE

When Darcy heard the knock on the door she frowned. Was it Cable, the hotel manager, or maybe Clint Adams? There was only one way to find out. She steeled herself to handle the situation in case it *was* Adams, but when she opened the door she saw that it was John Cable.

"Let me in, before somebody sees me," he said, rushing past her.

"You got my message," she said, closing the door after him.

"About Adams? Yeah, I got it. We all met and talked it over. We're trying to come up with a plan to handle him."

"Handle him? That doesn't mean kill him, does it?"

"No," Cable said. "You know me better than that. I'm not going to kill an innocent man to protect our operation, Darcy. I'd call it off first."

Darcy looked relieved and said, "Good. Hey, if you're here, who's across the street?"

"Mack."

She made a face.

"Why was he included in this?"

"He's a good man."

"I don't like him."

"Neither do I, but he'll do his job."

Cable sat in the armchair while Darcy sat on the bed.

"What if this doesn't work, Cable?" she asked. "I mean, Adams is a complication, but what if the plan just doesn't work?"

"We want Lyle Jason, right?"

"Right."

"And what's his weakness?"

"Whores."

"And our thoughts were that the bigger the whore, the more interest, right?"

She gave him an exasperated look.

"I know what our plan was, Cable," Darcy said. "It doesn't seem to be working, does it?"

"Well, not yet, Darcy," Cable said, "but when presented this plan we knew we'd be in it for the long run."

"I know."

Cable walked to the window and looked out, then turned to face her.

"Darcy, do you want out?" he asked. "Is it too much for you?"

"No," Darcy answered quickly, "of course not. I'm ready to go through with this."

"Maybe it's too much?" he asked. "I mean . . ." He waved his arms. "This?"

She knew what he meant. He was suggesting that maybe the part of being with the men was too much for her. Little did he know that was the easy part. Besides, most of the time the men who came up to her room were sent by Cable.

"No, it's not too tough, Cable," she said. "I can handle it."

"Then what is it?" he asked. "Adams?"

She made a face.

"That was a bad idea, wasn't it?" she asked. "Using his name?"

"I guess so."

"I'm not blaming you," she said. "We decided together whose name would be impressive."

"I know."

"And now he's here, in Denver," she said, laughing without humor. "What are the odds?"

"I guess not as long as we thought."

He walked to her and sat down next to her on the bed.

"Don't worry, Darc," he said. "We won't let him get to you."

"I know you'll try not to," she said, "but after all, he is who he is."

"Darcy, I swear—"

"What if I should talk to him?"

"What?"

"I mean, where's the harm in what he did?" she asked. "I'm sure he's above that kind of ... ego, don't you think?"

Cable sat back.

"Not if he's a man."

She looked at him.

"You mean you would react badly if you heard a rumor like that about you?"

"Well, not me," Cable said, "but then I'm a man unlike any other man."

"Oh, I know that," she said. "You've told me that plenty of times."

"Don't you believe me?"

"Sure," she said. "Every time you tell it to me, I believe it."

He smiled at her and said, "You can find out for yourself, you know . . . anytime you want."

She smiled back, patted his knee, and said, "I'll keep that in mind."

She stood up.

"If you're going to keep the Gunsmith away from me maybe you better get to it."

He stood up.

"I guess I should."

They walked to the door together.

"Maybe you're just going a little stir-crazy in this room," Cable suggested. "Would it help to get out for a while?"

"Well, once we take care of the Clint Adams problem maybe I will," she said.

"I'll take care of it."

"I'm not altogether convinced that I shouldn't just talk to him and explain everything to him."

"Everything?" Cable asked. "The plan and all?"

"I guess not," Darcy said. "Don't listen to me. I'm just talking."

As Cable left the room they were both thinking that it was "just talking" that had gotten them into this.

THIRTEEN

Denver scared Earl Terry. He was so used to open spaces that he felt cramped. It was almost as if he couldn't breathe. It wasn't until he and Jason came to a park that he was able to take a deep breath.

Lyle Jason had taken him out and shown him Denver the day before, and then again last night. Now Jason was making him walk around in the morning, after breakfast. It was close to lunchtime when they came to the park.

"It's great, ain't it?" Jason asked.

"Yeah," Terry said, "great." He wasn't even sure exactly what Jason was talking about. He mopped the sweat from his brow with a handkerchief. He couldn't stop sweating whenever they left the hotel.

"What's the matter, Earl?"

"It's warm."

It wasn't warm, but Jason didn't call Terry on it. He recognized fear when he saw it. In fact, he liked seeing fear on the faces of others. It was interesting to discover that his partner's fear was included.

He clapped Terry on the back and said, "Let's find a restaurant. Even the food in the city is different."

"Okay."

They started away from the park and Terry thought, How different could the food be? At least if they were sitting in a restaurant eating he could pretend that they were someplace else.

God, he wished they were someplace else!

Earlier that morning, Clint finished eating his breakfast and ordered another pot of coffee. He sat back and looked up at the ceiling. Someplace in this building was the woman who was, for some reason, defaming his manhood.

God, he felt silly even thinking about it. He couldn't imagine he had come this far just to confront some woman who claimed to have slept with him. He'd faced all kinds of adversaries in the past and had met most of them with his gun. Not this time, though. You couldn't shoot a woman for saying you were bad in bed, could you?

He looked up and saw Talbot Roper enter the dining room. He waved his hand until Roper saw him and came over.

"Morning, Clint."

"Tal. Pull up a chair and have some coffee."

"Thanks."

A waiter brought another cup, and Roper poured it full and sat back.

"What brings you here?" Clint asked.

"I found your girl."

"Already?"

Roper nodded around a sip of coffee.

"She's in this hotel, right?"

"Right."

"What room?"

"Room 312."

Clint stared at him.

"You already got the room number?"

"Yes."

"Great," Clint said, pushing his chair back.

"No, hold it, don't leave," Roper said, waving Clint back into his chair.

"Why not?"

"There's more."

"Like what?"

"Something's going on."

"Like what?" Clint asked again.

"I'm not sure."

"Then why do you say something's going on?"

"Because there's a lot of men around her, watching her."

Clint stared at his friend for a moment.

"Isn't she supposed to have men around her? I mean, isn't she a whore?"

"No, not those kind of men."

"What kind then?" Clint asked. "Why are you making me drag this out of you?"

"Okay, look," Roper said, "somebody's watching her from the building across the street. I have a contact in the hotel who says there's a new bellboy working here."

"So?"

"He started at the same time she checked in."

"You said men. Just the two?"

"No," Roper said, "I think somebody's got a surveillance on her, because there are two or three men watching from across the street, at different times. They switch off."

Clint frowned.

"What's going on?"

"I don't know."

"Why would somebody be watching a whore?"

"She's not really calling herself a whore," Roper said.

"What does she call it?"

"I don't know, but it's not whore. I mean, she doesn't work the street. Men go up to her room."

"And how does she meet these men?"

"I don't know. She rarely leaves the room."

"How does she do business if she doesn't leave the room?" Clint asked.

"Maybe somebody's sending them to her?"

"So she has a pimp."

"Not that I can see," Roper said, "but I can keep looking."

"Maybe you can find out who's watching her," Clint said.

"Is that what you want me to do?"

Clint thought a moment, then said, "I guess so."

"Why?" Roper asked.

"She might be in danger."

"You don't even know the woman, Clint," Roper said, "plus she's been spreading rumors about you."

"I know," Clint said, "but that doesn't mean I want her to die."

"Are you going to talk to her?"

"Yes."

"When?"

"I don't know," Clint said. "I guess I'll have to think about it for a while."

"Well," Roper said, pushing his chair back, "then I'll get to work and see if I can find out what's going on."

"Okay," Clint said. "Talk to you later."

Clint watched Roper leave the dining room, marveling at what the man had managed to find out in less than a day. That's why he was generally acknowledged as the best in his business.

Now he was faced with a dilemma. Originally all he'd wanted was to talk to this woman. Now it appeared as if she was being watched. For what purpose? If he went up to her room now to talk to her, what would he be walking into?

Later that day, after lunch, Lyle Jason asked Earl Terry, "What's the name of the hotel that woman is supposed to be staying in?"

"The Denver House."

"I know where that is," Jason said. "Let's go and take a look."

The only place Terry wanted to go was to their hotel to pack, and then to the train station to get out of Denver, but he said, "Okay."

FOURTEEN

"Aren't we going in?" Terry asked Jason.

"Not yet."

They were down the block from the Denver House hotel, standing in a doorway.

"What are we doing here?"

"We're waiting," Jason said, "and watching."

"For what?"

"I don't know."

"Then how will we know when we see it?"

Jason looked at Terry.

"I'll know," he said, and looked back at the hotel. "Right now I want you to go across the street and find your own doorway."

"What for?"

"Because both of us standing in this one is a little conspicuous, Earl,'' Jason said. "Don't you think?''

"Sure, Lyle,'' Terry said, "whatever you say. Uh, what do I do when I find one?''

"Just keep an eye on the front door of the hotel and remember what you see,'' Jason said, "and don't leave until I come and get you. Have you got that?''

"I've got it.''

"Good,'' Jason said, "then go.''

Lyle Jason did not watch as Earl Terry crossed the street and found a doorway, as he was told to do. He knew that Terry would obey. He kept his eyes on the hotel, and the street in front of it, because he never rushed into anything without checking it out first. That was how he had managed to go on so long, doing what he'd been doing, without getting caught.

And he'd been doing it a long time.

Clint was so unsure as to what to do that he just hung around the hotel that afternoon. He spent some time in the hotel bar, and the rest of the time he was in the lobby, watching the people, reading a newspaper, or just sitting.

During one of the periods when he was people-watching he noticed the man he knew to be the hotel manager, a man named Roulet. The manager would come out and stand behind the desk and look at Clint nervously. No one else in the lobby seemed nervous, just the manager, and the cause of his nervousness seemed to be Clint.

Clint thought that this was probably something that he should check out.

There was something else, though. Another man seemed interested in him, although this one was not displaying any nerves. One of the bellhops appeared to be watching him. What made the man interesting was that he didn't seem to be doing his job. At one stretch the man went a half an hour without carrying one bag, and the hotel manager never said a word to him.

Strange behavior from two men who seemed to have one

thing in common—an interest in Clint Adams.

Clint was sure that this bellman was the one Talbot Roper had told him about. What he had to decide was whether or not he wanted to brace the man, or leave the task to Roper.

He finally decided to start with the hotel manager. The next time the man appeared behind the desk, Clint stood up and walked over to talk to him.

"Mr. Roulet?"

Clint was certain the man had seen him walking over, and was studiously avoiding looking at him. Having been addressed directly, though, the man had no choice but to respond.

"Ah, yes, Mr. Adams. How nice to see you with us again."

"I wonder if we might talk?"

The prospect seemed to push the man from nervous to frightened.

"Oh, ah, I don't know if I can—"

"It won't take long."

"I'm very busy—"

"I insist."

The man started to sweat.

"Oh, very well, then. Please come to my office."

Roulet came out from behind the desk and conducted Clint to his office. The rather portly manager sat behind his desk and regarded Clint with obvious trepidation. What did he think was going to happen?

"H-how can I help you?"

"Why are you so nervous?"

"Nervous?"

"Yes," Clint said, seating himself across from the man. "When someone sweats the way you are now, it usually means they're nervous."

"I—uh—don't know—uh—"

"You've been watching me all day, too," Clint said.

"Would this have anything to do with the woman in room 312?"

"Oh, God—" the man said, surprising Clint.

"Mr. Roulet," Clint asked, "what is going on?"

"I did not mean to—to—"

"To what?"

"It is only that she told me—uh, that she slept with you—and, I, uh . . ."

"Go on."

"Are—are you here to k-kill me?"

Ever since he'd had sex with Darcy Flanders, Roulet knew that this day would come. He never should have told anyone what she said about the Gunsmith's prowess in bed, but he was just an ordinary man and he'd had to brag to someone. He'd only told two friends that she told him that he was better than Clint Adams in bed, and that Clint Adams—the Gunsmith—was not that good. Soon the story got back to him, and then he knew that it would probably spread and spread until the Gunsmith himself heard it and came here to kill him.

"Kill you for what reason?"

"Are you here to kill *her*?" Roulet was puzzled.

"Mr. Roulet," Clint said, "I'm not here to kill anyone." That seemed to puzzle the manager.

"Then why are you here?"

"I'm here to talk."

"Just talk?"

"Yes."

"With me?"

"With the woman in 312," Clint said, "Darcy Flanders. It seems she has been spreading some rumors about me, and to tell you the truth, I don't recall ever having met a woman by that name."

Roulet stared across his desk at Clint.

"You've never met her?"

"Not by that name," Clint said. "Does she go by another?"

"I, uh, don't know."

"Can you describe her?"

The man did so, and in such glowing terms that Clint knew that he was either in love with her, or he'd slept with her, or both.

"She sounds very beautiful," Clint said.

"Oh, she is," Roulet said, "and very accomplished."

Yes, the man had slept with her.

"Tell me, why would you—the manager of a prestigious hotel like the Denver House—allow this woman to do business from one of your rooms?"

"Uh, do business?"

"Well," Clint said, "she is a whore, isn't she?"

"My dear sir, whatever gave you that idea?" Roulet asked.

"Don't cover for her, Mr. Roulet," Clint said. "The word is out and you know it."

"As I said before," Roulet said in his own defense, "she is very beautiful, and very accomplished."

"Would the owners of this hotel accept that as a reason, I wonder?" Clint said.

"The, uh, owners?"

"Yes," Clint said. "Have they heard the stories yet?"

"The owners are, uh, not from Denver," Roulet said. "I doubt they have heard, uh, anything."

"Would you like them to hear everything?"

"No . . . no, I would not," Roulet said.

"Then perhaps you should tell *me*," Clint suggested, "everything you know. . . ."

FIFTEEN

Pierre Roulet did indeed tell Clint Adams everything he knew, which wasn't much. He told Clint when Darcy Flanders had arrived, he told him the effect she'd had on everyone, himself included.

"You slept with her."

He had *not* been going to tell Clint that, but when asked directly he admitted that yes, he had.

"Once."

"Because she wanted you to let her stay?"

Roulet struggled for an answer and then simply shrugged helplessly.

"I am, after all, only a man," he said.

"And French."

"Ah," Roulet said, "you understand."

"Perhaps."

"You will understand more, my friend, when you see her."

"I'm sure I will."

"Well, if that is all—" the hotel manager said, starting to rise.

"No," Clint said, "that is not all, Mr. Roulet."

Roulet sat back down heavily.

"But . . . what else is there?"

"You have a bellboy here who is not doing his job."

"Then he shall be fired," Roulet said. "Just tell me who he is."

"You know who he is," Clint said. "You saw him today."

"I can assure you," the manager said, "if I saw such a man he would be fired."

Clint studied the man for a few moments. Was it possible he was telling the truth? Could it be that he was so nervous about Clint that he hadn't noticed the inactive bellboy?

"I will talk to the desk clerks and see if you are right, Mr. Adams," Roulet said. "If you are, he will be fired."

"Don't do that, Mr. Roulet."

"Why not?"

"I have a feeling he shouldn't be fired, not just yet. At least, not until I can find out what he is doing here."

"Very well, then," Roulet said.

"Tell me, has anyone else been interested in Miss Flanders?"

"Monsieur—" Roulet gave him a knowing look.

"No, I don't mean for professional reasons. Has anyone been trying to find out her room number unsuccessfully, as I did?"

"I will have to check."

"Please do it, and let me know."

"I will, monsieur."

"Thank you."

"Monsieur Adams, please allow me to apologize."

"For what?"

"For passing on what information Miss Flanders gave me," the manager said. "I had no idea she was lying to me. She is, uh . . ."

"Very accomplished," Clint finished for him. "Yes, so you said. It's all right, Mr. Roulet. I just ask one thing of you, as a long and valued guest at the Denver House hotel."

"Anything, monsieur."

"Don't tell her about this conversation."

"I would not dream of it," Roulet said. "In fact, I was going to put her out of the hotel."

"No, don't do that."

"Why not?"

"Because something is going on and I want to find out what it is."

"Monsieur . . . are my guests in some kind of danger?" the man asked.

"I don't know, Mr. Roulet," Clint said. "That's what I want to find out."

"Perhaps I should call for the police?"

"And tell them what?" Clint asked. "That Darcy Flanders lied to you? I doubt they'll find that actionable. No, just give me a couple of days. Don't do anything until you hear from me, not about Miss Flanders, and not about the bellboy I mentioned."

"Very well," Roulet said. He had completely regained his composure and was being very professional. "I shall leave the matter in your hands."

"Thank you for your cooperation, Mr. Roulet."

SIXTEEN

Lyle Jason was not a stupid man. He hadn't survived this long by being stupid. He was also a very observant man. It was for this reason that he was able to determine that someone was watching the hotel from a third-floor window right across the street. He could see the man in the window, doing nothing but watching and occasionally eating something.

Some hours later he saw that there was a different man in the window, but no one had come out or gone into the building by the front entrance. That meant that they must have changed places by using a back way.

After determining that this was going on, he crossed the street and found Earl Terry in a doorway.

"Come on, Earl."

Terry actually didn't want to leave his doorway. He felt

safe there and hadn't minded spending better than four
hours there.

"Where are we going, Lyle?" he asked.

"We're going to find out what the hell is going on
around here," Jason said.

Will Blake turned away from the window when he heard
the knock at the door.

"What?" he called.

The knock again. No one had knocked on the door before
because they all had keys. Dave Selby was due to relieve
him, and Blake assumed the man had lost his key.

"Okay, I'm coming."

He walked to the door and opened it.

"What happened?" he asked. "Forget—"

He was interrupted by a huge hand that lashed out and
closed around his throat. In moments Blake was slumping
to the floor, dead.

"Drag him away from the door," Jason instructed Earl
Terry, who was still holding the man by the neck, even
though he was prone on the floor.

Terry grabbed the man's belt and carried him by belt and
throat away from the doorway. Lyle Jason closed and
locked the door behind him.

He walked to the fallen man, examined him, and cursed.

"What's wrong?" Terry asked.

"I didn't tell you to kill him."

"I guess I squeezed too hard."

"I guess so."

"Who is he?"

"I can't ask him that, can I?" Jason said.

"I'm sorry, Lyle—"

"Forget it," Jason said, "we'll just have to stay here
and wait for the next one."

"How did you know he was here?"

"I saw him from the street."

"And there are more?"

"At least one more."

"What are they doing?"

Jason waved and said, "They're watching the hotel."

"Why?"

"I don't know that, Earl," Jason said. "That's why we're going to stay here and wait for the next man to come along. We're going to ask him."

"When will he be here?" Terry asked.

"I don't know. It may be a matter of hours—"

At that moment there was the sound of a key being fit into the lock.

"—or now," Jason said. "Move to the side of the door, grab him when he comes in, but don't kill him!"

"Right."

Earl Terry did as he was told, and as the man entered the room he grabbed him from behind, pinning his arms to his sides.

"What the—"

Jason stepped forward and relieved the man of his gun.

"Okay, Earl," he said, "let him go and shut the door."

Terry released Dave Selby, who rubbed his arms and stared across the room at the fallen Will Blake.

"Will?"

"He can't answer you," Jason said.

"Is he dead?"

"He can't get any deader."

Selby focused on Jason, sensing that this was the man in charge. As he stared at the man, it started to dawn on him who he was. When he looked at Earl Terry and saw the size of him, he realized who the two men were, but he kept quiet about the realization.

"Who are you?"

Jason covered the man with his own gun.

"I think I'll be asking the questions, friend," Jason said. "Why are you watching the Denver House hotel?"

Selby thought fast and came up with what he thought was a plausible answer.

"I was hired to."

"By who?"

"A woman."

"Why?"

"Her husband."

Jason frowned.

"Are you telling me that you're a private investigator?"

"That's right."

"You're watching a cheating husband?"

Selby nodded.

Jason looked around the room, which he hadn't had a chance to do yet.

"Watch him," he said to Terry, who drew his gun and pointed it at Selby.

Jason walked around. From the looks of the place, the two men and perhaps more had been using it for at least a week, maybe longer.

"How many men?" he asked Selby.

"Just me and . . . my partner."

"What's your name?"

Selby hesitated just a moment before giving his real name.

"And what was his?"

"Blake."

"What's the name of your agency?"

Now he knew he was in trouble. If he said something like "Selby/Blake" it could be checked.

"We're with the Pinkertons."

Jason whirled on the man and glared at him. Selby shrank back from the look. Terry was the huge, imposing man, Jason the smaller man, but it was the look in Jason's eyes that was the scary one.

"Oh, I think you just made a very big mistake, my friend."

"H-how . . ."

"The Pinkertons wouldn't assign one man to a wayward husband, let alone two or—the way it looks here—more.

See, they've got more important things to do."

"The, uh, woman is very wealthy," Selby tried. "She's, uh, real important."

He noticed that Jason was shaking his head, not believing him.

"I think we'll try this again, my friend," Jason said, "and if I don't get answers I can live with, then *you* won't live with them. Understand?"

"I understand."

"So," Jason said, "why are you watching the Denver House hotel? . . ."

SEVENTEEN

"He spotted me."

Cable looked at Ron Wilson and frowned.

"How could he spot you?" he asked. "Why would he even suspect you?"

"I don't know," Wilson said. "Maybe he's as good as his reputation."

"His reputation is with a gun."

"And with women," Wilson said. "Don't forget that."

"Whatever," Cable said. "Neither of those things would help him spot you—unless you were careless."

"I wasn't."

Cable wasn't sure about that. Wilson might not have been the best choice to play the bellboy. Cable doubted that the man did much heavy lifting.

"And there's another thing."

"Now what?" Cable asked.

"The manager, Roulet? He was asking about me today."

"Asking what?"

"He was asking the desk clerk if I was doing my job properly."

"And have you been?"

Wilson looked away.

"Ron?"

"Well, I couldn't very well watch Adams and carry bags up and down the stairs, could I?"

"Now I get it," Cable said. "You screwed up. Adams noticed that you weren't doing your job."

"I'm doing *my* job by keeping an eye on him."

"You've got to do your *bellboy* job to keep your cover," Cable said.

"I told you in the beginning I didn't *want* to be the bellboy."

They were standing in a hallway behind the hotel kitchen. Wilson had let Cable in a back door.

"You better get back to it before somebody notices you're gone," Cable said.

"Fine."

"If Adams approaches you, play dumb."

"I know!" Wilson said testily.

And it would be easy for him, Cable thought.

When the man was out of sight, he found the back stairs to the upper levels and went up to talk to Darcy.

The bellboy knew.

Clint was sure that the man now knew that he was being watched—or watched *back*. He wondered what Roulet had done to tip him off.

Maybe the best thing to do now would be to talk to him, but suddenly the man had disappeared. Could it be that he'd left and abandoned whatever job it was he was doing?

Clint decided to sit in the lobby for another half hour to

see if the bellboy appeared again. If he didn't, then he'd decide what to do at that point.

Shane Mack fit his key into the lock, turned it, and opened the door. Immediately, he knew something was wrong. It was too quiet. Whether it was Selby or Blake he was relieving, they always had something smart or sharp to say when he arrived, especially if he was late, like tonight. He'd met a girl, though, a waitress at one of the restaurants in the area, and he'd not only been sleeping with her, but staying with her. Tonight Marion had been especially eager and had kept him in bed past the time he was supposed to relieve Selby.

Little did Mack know at the time that his girlfriend's sexual appetite had saved his life.

He entered the room and saw the two bodies. Blake was crumpled against a wall, but it was Selby's body that made the blood drain from his face. Somehow, whoever had killed him had nailed him, spread-eagled, to the wall. There was no blood, and from the position of the head Mack figured his neck was broken.

Without checking the two bodies, Mack backed out of the room and got away from there fast. The location was no longer secure, and procedure called for him to get away and stay alive.

He was very good at following procedure when it called for him to stay alive.

Clint saw the man enter the hotel lobby in an agitated condition. In fact, the man was as pale as if he'd seen a ghost. He paused just inside to look around. At that moment the bellboy appeared again—finally—and the man headed right for him.

Clint watched the exchange between the two men with interest. The bellboy looked shocked by what the other man had to tell him, and turned to point behind him. Clint couldn't see what he was pointing at, and assumed he was pointing at something out of sight—perhaps referring to another person.

Finally, both men headed for the stairs and went up to the second or third floor.

What the hell was going on?

EIGHTEEN

Cable and Darcy didn't have much time to say anything before there was an urgent knock on the door. Darcy opened it, and both Shane Mack and Ron Wilson came barreling in.

"They're dead!" Mack said, out of breath and pale.

"What?" Darcy said.

"Who's dead?" Cable asked.

"Both of them!"

"Both of who?" Cable asked.

"Shane," Darcy said, "calm down and tell us what you're talking about."

"Selby and Blake," Mack said, "are both dead."

"What?" Darcy said.

"I walked in to relieve Selby and he...he's on the wall!"

"What do you mean, he's on the wall?" Cable asked.

Mack explained what he had found when he walked in, and the horror showed on all their faces—even Wilson's, and he had heard it down in the lobby.

"Who would do that?" Darcy asked.

"Who else?" Cable said.

"You think it was Jason?" she asked.

"Who else?" he said again. "What did you do, Mack?"

"I got out of there."

"You left him hanging on the wall?" Darcy asked.

"Hey," Mack said defensively, "I followed procedure."

"For once," Darcy said.

"Listen—" Mack started.

"Hey, forget it, you two," Cable said. "Let's stop arguing among ourselves and decide what to do."

"We pull out, that's what we do," Ron Wilson said.

"No," Shane Mack said, "we call for help."

"I think the first thing we have to do is get Selby down from that wall," Darcy said.

"Hey, I acted according to procedure—" Mack started again, but Cable cut him off.

"We know that, Shane," he said, "but what Darcy is suggesting is that we go against procedure."

"What if that's what he wants?" Mack asked. "What if he's just waiting for us to try it?"

"What of it?" Cable asked. "There'll be four of us."

"Come on, Cable," Darcy said, "let them stay here if they want to."

She headed for the door and Cable followed.

"Well," Mack said to Wilson, "they've got a point about one thing."

"What?"

"There would be four of us, if we all went."

They looked at each other, then around at the empty room, then hurried to catch up with Darcy and Cable.

Clint watched with interest as a woman and a man came
hurrying down the steps to the lobby, followed closely by
the bellboy and the other man. Not a firm believer in coincidence, he was convinced that this was Darcy Flanders.
He didn't have a guess as to who the men were, but they
were obviously with her. That meant she was not only being watched, but she had men around her as well.

They hurried through the lobby and outside. Clint got up
and went to the door. He watched them cross the street. He
looked around the lobby and saw that no one was paying
any attention to him. He left the hotel and started after the
four people.

They moved quickly down the block and around the corner, and he followed, but not too closely. It soon became
obvious that they were working their way around to the
back of the building that was across the street from the
hotel. The area behind the building was like a big empty
lot, so there wasn't anyplace for him to hide closer to the
building. He watched as they went in a back door, and then
he found another doorway and settled in to wait and see
what happened.

NINETEEN

"Jesus Christ," Darcy said, covering her mouth with her hands, "get him down."

"Come on," Cable said, and he and Wilson and Mack pried Selby from the wall and set him on the floor. Nails had been driven through his hands and feet to secure him to the wall.

"Where'd they get the nails?" Wilson wondered aloud. "And the tools?"

"They couldn't have brought them with them," Cable said. "This had to be a spur-of-the-moment decision."

"To send us a message," Darcy said.

"Well, we got it," Cable said, standing up straight but looking down at Selby. "Jason's here, and Earl Terry's with him."

"How do you know that?" Wilson asked.

"Both Selby and Blake have broken necks," Cable said. "That's Terry's trademark."

"We've got to get help," Wilson said.

"Are you kidding?" Cable said. "Do you know what I had to do to get the six of us assigned? They'll never give us more men."

"Don't they want Jason?" Mack asked.

"Not as badly as we do," Darcy said.

Mack was aware that catching Lyle Jason had become something very personal for both Cable and Darcy, but he didn't know why.

"Do you want us to go ahead with it?" Wilson asked. "Even though Jason knows we're here?"

Darcy and Cable exchanged a glance, and a nod.

"Darcy and I are going ahead," Cable said. "It's up to you if you want to stay or go."

"No hard feelings," Darcy said, "whatever your decision is."

"What's the point?" Mack asked. "He and Terry are probably on the next train out of here."

"No," Cable said, "I don't think so."

"Why not?" Wilson asked.

"Because Jason will take this as a challenge," Darcy said.

She looked at Cable and her look said, *And he wants me.*

"It's Darcy," Lyle Jason said.

They were back in their hotel room, and Earl Terry was relaxed for the first time.

"The Flanders woman?" he said. "What makes you think so?"

"Who else would try to set me up like this?" Jason asked. "Who else would be smart enough, and desperate enough?"

"What's going on between you two, anyway?" Terry asked.

Jason shook his head.

"Nothing I could explain to you, Earl. Let's just say it's a personal thing between me and the lady."

"But I'm here, too," Terry said.

"That's a personal thing between you and me, Earl," Jason said.

"So what are we going to do now?"

Jason reclined on the bed, his hands behind his head.

"Let's give them a chance to react to the situation," he said. "There's no rush."

There was a rush for Earl Terry, though. The sooner this was over, the sooner he could get away from Denver and back to a part of the country where he could have some space.

"Relax, Earl," Jason said, reading his partner's face, "it'll be over soon enough."

TWENTY

Clint waited as long as he could and then wondered if they'd gone out the front way. He decided to take a closer look rather than take a chance on losing them. He went inside, found the first and second floors empty, and went up to the third floor. He followed the sound of voices and stopped just outside an open door.

What he heard chilled him.

"I don't know how anyone could do that," Darcy said, unaware that Clint Adams was just outside the door. "I mean, killing someone is bad enough without nailing him to the wall."

"I wonder . . ." Shane Mack said, and then stopped.

"Wonder what?" Cable asked.

Mack looked around, aware that all three of them were watching him.

"I was just wondering if he was, uh, still alive when they nailed him to the wall."

"Oooh," Darcy said, putting her hand over her mouth.

"Sorry," Mack said with a helpless shrug. "I was just, you know, thinking."

"I don't think you were," Cable said. "Darc, you want to go back to the hotel? We'll take care of this."

"No," Darcy said, "I'm fine. Besides, I think we should all stay together, don't you?"

"I do," Cable said, then added, "that is, if we're all staying?"

He and Darcy looked over at Mack.

"Hell, yeah, I'll stay," Mack said. "Why not?"

"Wilson?" Cable asked.

"Not me," he said. "Hey, I was sent here to be a bell-boy, remember? This"—he waved his hand—"isn't in my job description."

"Fine," Cable said. "You can head back to Washington on the first train in the morning."

"I'll do just that."

The room got quiet for a few moments.

"Hey," Wilson said, "I'm not really an agent anyway, you know—"

"Forget it," Cable said.

"Nobody said nothing about nailing people to the wall," Wilson complained, "or about going up against the Gun-smith."

"We're not going up against him," Cable said, "we're going to try to avoid him. . . ."

"That ain't what it sounded like to me," Wilson said, "but either way I don't want any part of it. I'm leaving now, and I'm going to see if I can get a train back to D.C. today."

He headed for the door. The only reason he didn't hear

Clint scrambling down the hall was because Darcy shouted after him, "Wilson, come back! We've got to stay together."

Wilson went on without turning back. Clint just barely beat him out of the building and back to his doorway. He had to flatten himself against the door to try to make himself invisible, but he needn't have bothered. The man went right by without looking, his pace quickening with each step.

Clint stayed where he was, watching the back door, expecting the others to follow along soon. When they didn't appear, he decided to chance going back up.

"What do we do now?" Mack asked. "There's only three of us."

"First thing we've got to do is get Blake and Selby out of here."

"Why?" Mack asked.

"They have to be buried."

"Cable, listen. That's only going to call more attention to us. We've got to leave them here."

"We can't do that," Cable said, "they have families—"

"When this is all over we can come back for them," Mack said. "Nobody will find them here."

"You're crazy," Cable said. "If that was you on the floor you'd want—"

"I'd be dead," Mack said, "and I wouldn't give a fart what you did with me." He looked at Darcy. "Tell your partner, Darcy, he'll listen to you."

Cable looked at Darcy.

"I hate to agree with him, Cable, but he's right."

"Not you, too—"

"Just listen," she said. "If we try to take the bodies out now, the police are going to get involved."

"Fine," Cable said, "they can help us—"

"You know that won't happen," she said. "They'll want to take over, and they'll want us to leave Denver. I'm not going to do that, Cable. Lyle Jason is mine.''

Cable stood with his hands at his sides, looking down at his fallen comrades.

Darcy walked up to him and put her hand on his arm.

''We'll come back for them, Cable,'' she said. ''I swear we will. Let's get Jason for what he did, first.''

Cable looked at her, then back at the bodies, then at Mack, who was staring out the front window, and then back at her.

''Okay, Darc,'' he said. ''Okay. We'll do it your way. We better get out of here.''

Once again Clint was just ahead as they left the building. Instead of hiding in his doorway he continued running and turned the corner as they came out of the building. He kept on going until he got back to the hotel.

TWENTY-ONE

Clint had dinner with Talbot Roper that night in the hotel dining room and told him what he'd found out.

"You know what that sounds like to me?" Roper said when Clint finished.

"Yeah, I do."

"What am I going to say?"

"Secret Service."

Roper looked surprised.

"That's exactly what I was going to say."

"Nobody else refers to their people as 'agents,' " Clint said.

"What the hell are the Secret Service doing going after someone like Lyle Jason?"

"What do you know about this Jason?"

"He's a killer, from what I hear," Roper said.

"Who's he killing?"

"Women."

"Women?"

"Prostitutes, or at least that's what I hear."

"So that explains why this woman, Darcy Flanders, would be set up in the hotel as a whore."

"Bait," Roper said.

"They were trying to make her noticeable enough to attract him."

"Put her in a big hotel," Roper said, "and mention the prominent men she's slept with."

"Including me."

"You should be flattered."

"If I had been," Clint said, "I never would have come here."

They finished off their dinners and had another pot of coffee.

"What do you want to do now?" Roper asked.

"What would you do?"

"I'd go home."

"Would you?"

"Yup," Roper said. "It's none of your business now."

"They did use my name."

"So let them know you know, you didn't like it, and then go home."

"This Jason," Clint said, "he didn't kill a woman today, he killed two men—and he nailed one of them to the wall."

Roper winced.

"You didn't know them, though."

"I think I'll send a telegram to D.C.," Clint said.

"That's right," Roper said, "you've done some work for the Secret Service in the past, haven't you?"

Clint nodded.

"Maybe Jim West can give you some information about these people."

"If he's around," Clint said. "If not, then I'll get it from someone else."

"Why are you doing this?"

"I just want to know something about these people before I decide what to do, Tal."

"Well," Roper said, "it's up to you." He stood up. "Do you think you'll need me anymore?"

"Something come up for you?"

Roper nodded.

"A case, but it'll take me out of town. If you need me, though, I'll turn it down."

"No, no," Clint said, "don't do that. You go ahead and conduct your business. I appreciate the help you've given me so far."

"I might only be gone a few days," Roper said. "When I get back I'll check in at the hotel and see if you're still here."

"Okay."

"Good luck, then."

"Watch your back." Clint knew that Roper usually worked alone.

"You, too."

After his friend left, Clint finished the pot of coffee on the table, then also left and went to find the nearest telegraph office. The hotel had its own telegraph key, but he didn't know who he could trust at the hotel. He preferred to go outside to send this particular message.

TWENTY-TWO

Earl Terry stood at the window of the hotel room, looking outside. He wished he had the nerve to pack and leave while Lyle Jason was out, but he knew he didn't. It wasn't that he was afraid of Jason. That wasn't it at all. The truth of the matter was he needed Lyle Jason. Earl Terry could not get along on his own. He needed Jason to tell him where to go and when. Terry had always needed someone to guide him, and Lyle Jason was the best guide he'd ever had—up to now. He had never eaten as well as he had with Jason, or lived as well, and all he had to do for Jason was kill someone from time to time.

Like yesterday afternoon. In fact, the three men he had killed yesterday was probably the most he had ever killed in one day. Well, in one afternoon, anyway. He remembered one time, when he was fifteen, when he killed more than that in one day, but they were teasing him. . . .

As big as Earl Terry had always been, he'd been told since he was a child what a tiny little mind he had. Now an adult in his early thirties, he still believed this, and was unable to think for himself.

Still, he wished he had the nerve to leave Denver. It was too big, with too many people, and it scared him.

Lyle Jason stood in a doorway across the street and down the block from the Denver House hotel. Ever since he'd seen Darcy Flanders for the first time yesterday, he couldn't get her out of his mind. Although she'd been trying to catch him for months, he had never gotten a good look at her until then. She was the most breathtakingly beautiful woman he had ever seen—and since he'd never seen a woman so beautiful, he'd never killed one so beautiful.

Darcy Flanders would be his masterpiece.

Darcy stood at her window, looking down at the street. From where she was—if she had known where to look— she would have seen Lyle Jason standing in his doorway, watching the hotel. Instead, she simply stared down at the street right below her window, thinking about the two dead men they had left in a room across the street. She recalled the horror she'd felt when they first entered the room and saw Selby hanging on the wall—*nailed* to the wall! How could someone do that?

She rubbed her upper arms, feeling a chill, and wondered if this would be the end of the line for Lyle Jason. Would Denver be the place she'd finally catch him and avenge the death of Laura? Or was this the place where she'd die trying?

Her partner, Cable, was the only person who knew about Laura. That was why he agreed to help her with what he called her "obsession."

"The faster we catch him and put him away," Cable had said, "the quicker you can get back to your regular life."

That was months ago—almost a year! A year out of their lives before they were finally able to come up with a plan they thought would draw him out.

Cable had gotten the other men to help, and now two of them were dead. Was it worth their lives to catch Jason?

The answer to that question was simple. If it was worth her life, it was certainly worth someone else's, and she had sworn that she would catch Lyle Jason, or die trying.

And she meant it.

Cable sat on the bed in his room at a cheaper hotel down the street. He thought back over the past months to the things he and Darcy had done to try to catch Lyle Jason. Now that they had him within their grasp, he wasn't sure he wanted her to be that close to the man. In fact, maybe Jason wasn't within their grasp, maybe they were within his.

Cable was determined not to let anything happen to Darcy. What he had to do was go out, find Jason, and take care of him without letting him get close to Darcy. What he didn't know was if he'd be able to take care of Lyle Jason alone.

He got up, pulled on his boots, slipped on his shoulder rig and jacket, and went out to find out.

TWENTY-THREE

Clint was in the lobby when the police arrived. There were two uniformed men flanking a third man, who was wearing a suit. They marched through the lobby to the front desk, where they talked with the desk clerk and then apparently asked to see the manager, Mr. Roulet. The Frenchman appeared moments later and took the man in the suit with him to his office. The two men in uniform remained in the lobby.

Curious, Clint walked to the desk.

"What's going on?" he asked the desk clerk.

The man looked around to see if anyone else was listening, took a quick glance at the two policemen, then leaned over the desk.

"They're asking about one of our bellmen, Ron Wilson."

"What about him?"

"He's dead."

"Really. How did that happen?"

"I'm not sure," the man said, "but it sounds to me like he was killed."

"Well," Clint said, "that's terrible. Did you know him?"

"Not real well," the desk clerk said. "He was kinda new, and to tell you the truth, he wasn't the best worker we ever had."

"Still," Clint said, "that'd be no reason to kill him, would it?"

"Hell, no," the desk clerk said, "poor bastard."

"Yeah," Clint said, "poor bastard."

He retreated to a lobby sofa, thinking about what Roper had told him about one of the bellmen. Combine that with the two dead men and it was just too much coincidence.

Clint made a spur-of-the-moment decision. First he was going to talk to Roulet after the police left, and then he decided he was going to talk directly to Darcy Flanders.

Once and for all he wanted to find out what was going on.

After about twenty minutes the policeman came back to the lobby. He met with the two uniformed men, then he left and the other two disappeared into part of the hotel, presumably to ask questions of some of the guests and employees.

Clint went to the front desk and asked to speak with Roulet.

"He's probably pretty upset right about now," the man said.

"He'll see me."

"Yeah," the clerk said, "sure, Mr. Adams. I'll tell him."

Clint waited a few moments before the desk clerk reappeared with the manager, who invited him back to his office.

"What can I do for you, Mr. Adams?"

"I wanted to know about your dead bellman."

Roulet stared at him.

"How did you find out so quickly?"

"Bad news travels fast, Mr. Roulet. What happened?"

"He was killed."

"How?"

The man shuddered.

"Apparently someone broke his neck."

"Where?"

"They are not sure, but he was found near the railroad station."

"Did they arrest anyone?"

"No," he said, "they do not have any suspects. They were asking me if I knew why anyone would want to kill him. How could I know that? I barely knew the man, myself. He was only working here a short while, and—" Roulet stopped short.

"And he wasn't very good at his job," Clint finished.

"He was the man you were telling me about, was he not?"

"It seems likely," Clint said, getting up to leave.

"Mr. Adams," Roulet said, "what is going on in my hotel?"

"That's what I'm going to find out, Mr. Roulet."

TWENTY-FOUR

Clint left Roulet's office, went up to room 312, and knocked on the door. After a moment, he knocked again.

"Who is it?" a woman's voice called out.

"Clint Adams."

There was another moment of silence and then the same voice asked tentatively, "*Who* is it?"

"Clint Adams, Miss Flanders. Would you open the door, please?"

Clint waited, wondering if he was going to have to knock again when finally he heard the lock turn and then the door opened.

He was struck by her beauty this close. Distance had diluted it when he saw her earlier, but now he was transfixed by it. Her hair was long and auburn, her skin flawless, her eyes a lovely green. He was also sure of one thing. He had never been to bed with her.

"You're Clint Adams?" she asked.

"Uh, yes, that's right."

"Should that mean something to me?"

"I think it should," he said, "since you claim that we've been to bed together."

"And who told you that?"

"How many people have you told?"

"Why are we having this conversation?" she asked.

"Because you started a rumor, Miss Flanders."

"What kind of—"

"I think we can move on, Miss Flanders. We have more important things to talk about."

"Really?" She was contriving to look uninterested. "Such as?"

"Two dead men," he said, "one of whom was apparently nailed to a wall."

She caught her breath, her eyes widening, and said, "You—"

"Not me," he said hurriedly. "I was outside in the hall when you and your three partners were taking him down."

"What—what do you want?"

"Well, for starters," he said, "I'd like to come in."

She hesitated.

"I'm not going to hurt you."

She thought a moment, then nodded and backed up to let him enter. He found himself in the large sitting room of a suite.

"What else do you know, Mr. Adams?" she asked. Her voice was more forceful now. She was trying to assume command of the situation.

"Miss Flanders, I came to Denver because of a silly rumor. I'm afraid my male ego brought me here, and that's not something I'm proud of. But now that I'm here I think perhaps you need help."

"As you yourself said, Mr. Adams," she replied, "I have three partners."

"I get the feeling you once had five, am I right?"

"Well, yes . . ."

"And yesterday you had three."

"Yesterday?"

"Yes," Clint said. "I don't know his name, but the man who was pretending to be the bellman?"

"Wilson."

"He's dead."

"What?" Her eyes widened again and she abandoned any pretense of being in charge. She groped for a chair, found one, and sat in it. He also sat down, across from her.

"Are you sure?"

"The police were just here. They told Mr. Roulet that he was killed near the train station."

"Oh, God," she said, "it's him. He was leaving."

Clint remembered now part of the conversation he had overheard, where the man had said he was going back to Washington.

"How was he killed?" she asked.

"Apparently his neck was broken."

He was surprised by her reaction. Her face turned red and she closed her hands into fists that were so tight they shook.

"Lyle Jason!"

"I've never heard of Jason," he said, "or this Earl Terry you mentioned."

She took a moment to focus her eyes and look at him.

"You were listening, weren't you?" she asked.

"Yes."

"What else did you hear?"

"I heard everything you said."

"Everything?"

They matched stares for a few moments and then he said, "I heard that you are all agents."

"And what does that mean to you?"

"Only one thing," he said. "Secret Service."

She frowned.

"I guess it could mean Pinkertons, but he tends to call his people operatives, not agents."

"What do you know about the Secret Service?" she asked.

"Enough. I've done some work for them."

She looked surprised.

"Really?"

He nodded.

"Jim West is a good friend, and William Masters Cartwright . . . well . . ."

"You're friends with the director?"

He smiled.

"Let's just say we know each other."

This seemed to make a difference to her.

"Mr. Adams, you might be right," she said. "Maybe we do need your help. Would you be willing to meet with me and my . . . my partners?"

"Sure, why not?" he said. "I came here to offer you my help, after all."

"Give me an hour, please," she said. "Are you staying here at the hotel—yes, of course you are."

"I'm in room 222."

"I'll contact you within the hour," she said.

Clint stared at her for a moment, wondering if she was telling him the truth, or if she was going to disappear on him.

"You don't believe me?"

"I sent a telegram to Washington."

"About what?"

"About you."

"What did you find out?"

"That you and your partner, John Cable, are a little headstrong. Neither of you has been with the Service very long, and you both have a habit of disobeying orders."

She frowned again.

"You do know somebody in Washington, don't you?"

"Yes."

"I know of Jim West's reputation, but I still haven't worked with him, or met him."

"You're in for a treat when you finally do," Clint said.

"Please believe me, Mr. Adams," she said. "More than ever I'm ready to accept your help. Just wait to hear from me."

"Within the hour," he said.

"Yes."

"Well," he said, standing up, "if I'm going to help you, I guess you'd better start calling me Clint."

TWENTY-FIVE

"You what?"

Cable glared at Darcy. Also sitting at the table in the restaurant with them was Shane Mack, but he was just a spectator for the moment.

"I talked with Clint Adams."

"Why the hell did you do that?"

"Because he came to my room."

"And you let him in?"

"What was I supposed to do, let him stand out in the hall?"

"Yes."

"He walked up to my door, bold as brass, knocked on it and announced himself."

"You still didn't have to open it."

"I wanted to hear what he had to say."

"And what *did* he have to say?"

Darcy gave them a brief rundown of her conversation with Clint.

"He knows West?"

She nodded.

"And Cartwright?" Mack asked, speaking for the first time.

"Yes."

"I've never met West," Cable said, almost pouting.

"Well, he has," she said. "In fact, it sounds like they're good friends."

"So? What does that mean? How did you leave it with Mr. Adams?"

"I told him I'd contact him in an hour."

"For what?"

"To set up a meeting."

"What kind of meeting?" Mack asked.

"Between the four of us."

"The four of us?" Cable asked. "Us and Wilson?"

"No, us and Clint Adams."

"What about Wilson?" Mack asked.

"Wilson's dead."

"What?" Mack said.

"How do you know that?" Cable asked.

"Clint Adams told me."

"And you believe him?" Cable asked.

"Why would he lie?" she asked. "Besides, I checked with the hotel manager before I left the hotel and he confirmed it. The police were there earlier today. Wilson was stopped before he could reach the train station. His neck was broken."

"Jason and Terry," Mack said.

"Right."

"So why are we having a meeting with Adams?" Cable asked.

"Because he's offered to help us."

"We don't need his help." Cable was sullen. He'd been

out most of the morning, determined that he was going to find Jason and save Darcy the trouble of having to deal with him, and he hadn't found a thing.

"We don't?" she asked.

"I agree with Cable," Mack said.

"Can I remind the two of you that once we were six, and now we're three?"

Both men remained silent.

"Lyle Jason and his boy, Earl Terry, have killed three of us," she said. "We need help, boys, and I think Clint Adams is just the one to give it to us."

"Maybe we should just leave Jason to Adams and go back to Washington ourselves," Mack suggested.

"That wouldn't work."

"Why not?" Mack asked.

"Because Jason is not Clint's problem, he's ours. Clint has simply offered to help."

"Clint?" Cable said.

"Adams," she said. "Mister, uh—Clint Adams."

"You're calling him Clint now?" Mack asked.

"Tell me something, Darcy?" Cable asked. "Why is Adams so anxious to help us—or is it you he wants to help, huh?"

"John Cable," she said, eyeing him dangerously, "if you weren't my partner I'd slap your face."

She stood up.

"Be in my room in one hour. Clint Adams will be there. If either of you—or both of you—is not there, I'll assume you've gone back to Washington."

With that she turned and left the restaurant, leaving both men to stare at each other blankly.

TWENTY-SIX

Clint got a message from Darcy to be in her room at five P.M. That was half an hour away. He wasn't in his room, but a bellboy had found him in the bar and given him the message.

He was working on a beer when the boy found him, trying to decide if he should get a quick bite to eat. Now he figured to finish the beer and then go up. While he was nursing the beer, a man entered and he recognized him as the policeman who wasn't in uniform, the one who had spoken to the manager. Clint had a feeling Roulet had given him up. His feeling was all but confirmed when the man started for his table.

"Clint Adams?" the man asked.

"That's right."

"My name is Lieutenant McBride, of the Denver police. I'd like to ask you a few questions."

"About what, Lieutenant?"

"An incident that happened sometime last night," the man said. "May I sit?"

"Sure, why not?" Clint said. "Can I get you a drink?"

"That won't be necessary."

McBride was not as old as Clint had first thought. When he'd entered the room he looked to be in his forties, but now he saw that it was the extra weight the man carried that made him look older. He was probably ten years younger than that, and if he lost forty pounds he'd look his age. Right now his face was heavy, and he was what could be generously called portly.

"How can I help you, Lieutenant?"

"A man was killed last night."

"That's terrible."

"Yes, it is," McBride said. "I know you by reputation, Mr. Adams. Death might be an everyday occurrence for a man like you—"

"I beg your pardon?" Clint said, cutting the man off.

"I mean to say, with the kind of life you lead and all, I know you—"

"You'll excuse me, Lieutenant," Clint said, "but I don't think you know a thing about the kind of life I lead. All you know is some nonsense you've read or heard. I would think, as a policeman, you wouldn't put much faith in that kind of information."

McBride stared at Clint for a few moments, obviously rethinking his approach.

"I'm, uh, sorry if I offended you, Mr. Adams," he said finally. "That was certainly not my intent."

"Well, it's what you accomplished, Lieutenant," Clint said, sounding more put out than he actually was. "It's an odd approach to take when you want to ask someone questions."

"As I said," McBride replied, "I apologize for, uh, being presumptuous. I would still like to ask you some questions about last night—"

"A man was killed," Clint said. "I only arrived in town a day or two ago, Lieutenant. I haven't had time to meet anyone."

"That may be the case," McBride said, "but we are questioning most of the guests and employees of the hotel, since the dead man was employed here."

Maybe Roulet hadn't given him up after all.

"Where did he work?" Clint asked.

"He was a bellboy."

"What was his name?"

"Ron Wilson."

Clint assumed a thoughtful pose for a long moment before speaking again.

"I really don't know the bellboys by name, Lieutenant. I don't know how I can help you."

The lieutenant regarded Clint silently for a few moments, as if trying to decide what approach to take.

"I spoke to the manager, Mr. Roulet."

"I guess you would."

"He mentioned to me that you had pointed out to him that one of the bellboys was not doing his job."

"Did I?"

"That's what he says."

"Then maybe I did," Clint said. "What about it?"

"It's possible that bellboy and the dead man are one and the same."

"Are you saying he was killed for not doing his job?" Clint asked.

"We don't know why he was killed, Mr. Adams," McBride said. "That's what we're investigating."

"I thought you were trying to find out who killed him?" Clint said, trying to confuse the man.

"Who and why are both part of the investigation, Mr. Adams."

"Well," Clint said, "I don't see how I can help you, Lieutenant."

"I was just wondering why you might have been watching this particular bellboy?"

"I can't say that I was, Lieutenant, and I won't call the manager a liar."

"I see."

"Is there anything else I can help you with?"

"Not at the moment." The man hesitated, then stood up. "Thank you for your time."

"Sure," Clint said. "Anything I can do to help."

"I may want to question you again at a later time," McBride said. "How long will you be in Denver?"

"I'm not sure," Clint said, "but like I said, I only just arrived, so I guess I'll be here at least a few more days."

"Well . . . again, thanks for your time and . . . I am sorry about . . . uh, insulting you."

"Thank you."

He watched while the lieutenant walked from the room, totally unimpressed with the man as a policeman. He wondered how he had managed to rise to the rank of lieutenant.

He finished the rest of his beer and then headed for room 312 again.

TWENTY-SEVEN

Darcy reacted immediately to his knock this time.

"Thanks for coming," she said, letting him in.

Clint entered and looked around.

"Aren't your partners going to be here?"

She closed the door and turned to face him, her hands clasped in front of her.

"To tell you the truth, I'm not sure."

"Why?"

Before she could answer there was another knock at the door.

"Maybe that's them." She hoped so. It would save her having to explain their absence.

She opened the door and both Cable and Mack were there.

"Glad you could make it," she said.

They both entered, looking a bit sheepish.

"Really," she said, touching Cable's arm and closing the door. "Clint, this is my partner, John Cable, and this is Shane Mack."

"Clint Adams," Clint said, extending his hand.

"Good to meet you," Cable said.

Mack simply shook hands.

"Why do I get the feeling we're all not happy I'm here?" Clint asked.

"Nonsense," Darcy said, "we're all grateful for your offer of help."

"And your eavesdropping," Mack said. "I don't suppose you told the police about . . . the dead men across the street?"

"No, I haven't."

"Why not?" Cable asked.

"It didn't seem appropriate—not that I didn't have the chance, though."

"What do you mean?" Darcy asked.

He explained how he'd been questioned by Lieutenant McBride about Ron Wilson.

"That's something I'm interested in," Cable said. "How did you know he was killed before we did?"

"Just lucky," Clint said. "I happened to be in the lobby when the police first got here, and I asked."

"Why don't we sit down?" Darcy suggested.

They all took seats.

"How do you know Jim West?" Cable asked.

"It's a long story," Clint said, "and not pertinent at all. Let's just say we've been friends a long time. Why don't we talk about the reason we're here?"

"Which is?" Mack asked.

"As I understand it, Lyle Jason?"

"That's right," Cable said, "and his partner, Earl Terry."

"What can you tell me about them?"

"They're killers," Mack said.

"They kill prostitutes."

Which explained why Darcy Flanders had set herself up as a high-class whore.

"They operate as one man," Darcy said. "Lyle is the brains, and Terry the brawn. He's a huge man, probably six eight or so."

"He apparently does whatever Jason tells him to do," Cable said.

"What's their relationship?"

The three Secret Service agents looked at each other.

"If you mean, how are they related, I don't think we know," Mack said.

"I think they're just partners," Darcy said.

"If they were partners," Clint said, "I don't think Jason would be telling Terry what to do all the time. It sounds more like Jason controls Terry."

"That may be the case," Darcy said.

"Why do we think they're still in town after killing three men?"

Cable and Mack looked at Darcy.

"I don't think he'll leave town until he gets me."

"Why is that?"

"I've been after him a long time," she said. "I think maybe he's finally decided to come after me."

"Why have you been after him so long?" Clint asked. "That's something I don't understand. Why is the United States Secret Service chasing a killer?"

"Well . . ." Darcy said, and neither of her partners jumped in to help her. "The truth of the matter is we're not really here . . . officially."

"What's that mean?"

"It's kind of personal," Darcy said. "You see, Jason and Terry killed my sister."

"Your sister was a prostitute?"

"I'm afraid so," Darcy said. "See, we went very different ways when our parents died. In fact, we were young and were split up. I went with one family, and my sister with another. We grew up very differently, and didn't find each other again until years later. By that time she was already a prostitute."

She stopped and the room got silent. Clint didn't know what to say.

"Well . . . I accepted her way of life, because she had no intention of changing. Then, about eight months ago, she was found dead in a hotel, her neck broken. When I looked into her death I discovered that it was one of a string of murders of prostitutes across the country."

"Further investigation revealed the killer to be Lyle Jason," Cable said, finally stepping in to help. "The only problem was, no one was able to catch him."

"So you decided to try?" Clint asked.

"I decided," Darcy said, "and Cable said he'd help."

"She's my partner."

Clint looked at Mack.

"Why are you here? And why were the others?"

They all looked at Mack and he said, "Would you believe stupidity?"

TWENTY-EIGHT

Cable and Mack left the room first. Cable stopped just outside the door.

"I don't feel comfortable leaving you with him," he said to Darcy.

"I'll be fine. I just want to fill him in some more," she explained.

"Yeah, okay."

"I'll talk to you later."

"Sure," he said. "Just be careful."

"I will."

She pushed him away and closed the door. When she turned, Clint was still seated in his chair, watching her.

"What?" she asked.

"Nothing."

"Why are you staring at me?"

"You don't know?"

She stared back for a few moments, then said, "Oh, that."

She walked back to her chair and sat down.

"What more can you tell me, Darcy?"

"About what? Or who?"

"About any of this," he said. "Have you ever actually seen Lyle Jason or Earl Terry?"

"No," she said. "I've never gotten that close."

"How convinced are you that they are the killers?"

"There's no doubt," she said. "That's why the Service has been giving me time to work on it."

"I wouldn't think Cartwright would be that understanding."

"Maybe he's mellowing."

Or maybe he's human after all, Clint thought, and susceptible to the charms of a beautiful woman.

"Jason has been identified in three different towns as the killer."

"How many women has he killed?"

"Over a dozen that we know of," she said. "There's probably a hell of a lot more."

"And Terry does the actual killing?"

"No," she said, "not when it comes to the girls, only when there's somebody else . . . like Selby and Blake."

"Are they the men who were killed across the street?" he asked.

"Yes."

"And Ron Wilson, was that the other man's real name?"

"Yes." She replied with her head down.

"Would you like to get a drink?" Clint asked.

"What?"

"A drink," Clint said. "I get the feeling you've been cooped up in this room for a long time."

"I have," she said. "It seems like forever."

"Why don't we go downstairs. I'll buy you a drink or two. Have you eaten dinner?"

"No," she said. "In fact, I didn't have any lunch and I'm kind of hungry."

"So am I. Why don't we have dinner?"

"Sure," she said, "why not? There's no point keeping up this pretense. I'm sure Jason's not fooled by it. I guess I was foolish to think he would be."

"Come on," he said, standing up, "we can talk more about it downstairs."

"Just give me a minute," she said, and went into the other room.

When she came out it was obvious that she had fixed her hair and face and put on some perfume.

"I'm ready."

"Let's go."

They left the room to go down to the dining room.

TWENTY-NINE

They got seated at a table and each ordered a steak dinner.

"Nothing like a steak," she said.

"I agree," he said. "Coffee?"

"Definitely."

The waiter brought a pot of coffee and poured them each a cup.

"How long have you been with the Secret Service?" Clint asked.

"About two years."

"And your partner?"

"Cable? Three."

"And neither of you have ever met Jim West?"

"The new kids don't get to work with the legends," she said.

"I guess not."

"You have, though," she said. "Haven't you?"

"Sure."

"What's he like?"

"Is that what we should be dealing with here, Darcy?" he asked.

She looked down into her coffee.

"No, I guess not."

"If Lyle Jason and Earl Terry are here in Denver," he said, "they're going to come after you, right?"

"That's what I think," she said, looking up at him. "I think it's all going to end here in Denver—for me, or for him."

"If not for him," Clint said, "then he'll just go on killing."

"Right."

"And if it ends for you . . . what?"

She shrugged.

"Maybe," she said, "eventually, I'll end up working with a legend."

"Maybe."

"Unless I already am."

"Meaning me?"

She shrugged.

"Aren't you some kind of legend?"

"Not to me, I'm not."

"No, I guess not," she said. "You're probably the only one who doesn't think so."

"I doubt it. Look, let's not talk about me, let's talk about you and your partners. What are you planning to do?"

"Well, as far as I'm concerned, I'm not leaving Denver until I get Jason."

"And Terry?"

"Jason will do."

"Why just him?"

"Because Terry's his weapon," she said. "Like a gun.

He points him, that's all. Besides, it was Jason who killed my sister."

"What about the other men? Selby and Blake?"

"All right, it was probably Terry who killed them. He'd be strong enough to nail Selby to the wall. But I still think it was Jason who told him to do it."

"You're probably right," he said. "I've known men like that before."

"Like Jason? Or Terry?"

"Both," he said. "Men like Jason like control, and they prey on men like Terry, who need someone to control them."

"You sound like you know what you're talking about."

"Sometimes I do."

"Yeah, well," she said, "I haven't felt that way in a long time."

"How did you get Mack and the others to go along with you, then?"

"I got Cartwright to go along with me."

"So you said. I still find that hard to believe."

"He's not so bad."

"It must be a personality thing, then."

"Yours or his?"

"Both," he said. "I guess we just clash."

"I think Mack is staying to get on Cartwright's good side," she said. "Wilson, he was heading back when he was killed."

"And the other two?"

"They had their reasons, I guess," she said. "I doubt they were good enough to die for, though."

At that point the waiter came with their dinners. They waited until he served and left to continue.

"Can you help me, Clint?" she asked. "Can you help me get Jason?"

"There only seems to be one way to do it."

"What's that?"

"Hold up here until he comes for you."

"And if he doesn't come?"

"There's no way we can find him, Darcy," he said, "not unless he kills some other girl while he's here, but I can't see him taking that kind of a chance, can you?"

"No."

"Then again," Clint went on, "coming after you would also be taking a chance."

"That one I think he'll take."

"Why?"

"He must know by now that I won't stop," she said. "I don't think he's a stupid man, just crazy."

"Maybe not even that."

"What else could he be? He's a cold-blooded killer."

"You don't have to be crazy to be a killer."

"Really? I always thought it was a prerequisite."

"Who told you that? I've known sane men who simply liked to kill."

"Do you?" Before he could answer, she went on quickly. "I'm sorry. I had no right to ask that."

"Forget it. Darcy, all you know about me is what you've heard or read. Even if half of that is true, it's still exaggerated."

"All right," she said. "I accept that."

While they were cutting into their steaks he asked, "Can you count on Cable and Mack?"

"Cable, yes," she said. "He's my partner and we count on each other."

"All right, what about Mack?"

"He's out for himself," she said. "I guess I can count on him to do anything that will benefit him."

"Fair enough," Clint said. "As long as you know where you stand you're ahead of the game."

They fell silent for a while to take care of their hunger. Afterward he asked, "How about that drink?"

"A beer would do fine."

Clint had the waiter bring two beers to the table.

"I've thought of another way to go," she said.

"And what's that?"

"Making myself visible," she said. "Going out onto the street."

"Painting a target on your back."

She nodded.

"I wondered if you'd come up with that," he said.

"It would draw him out," she said. "Staying in the hotel might discourage him."

Clint didn't answer. He was thinking.

"Well, what do you think?"

He shook his head.

"That puts the odds squarely in his favor," Clint said. "He could be on a roof with a rifle and we'd never be able to protect you."

"But you'd get him," she said. "Even if he killed me, you'd get him."

"Maybe, maybe not," Clint said. "Not if he made the kill from a distance. The only way for us to have a chance of catching him is by making him go after you in an environment we control."

She shook her head and said, "You really sound like you know what you're talking about."

"I've done this kind of thing before."

"Successfully?"

He drank down the last of his beer, then looked her straight in the eye and said, "Not always."

THIRTY

Clint walked Darcy back to her room, where they paused at the door.

"Would you like to come in?" she asked.

He wasn't sure what she meant by the offer, and decided she was just trying to be polite.

"I think I'll go down to the bar for a while and do some thinking," he said.

"Yes," she said, "I need to do some thinking alone, too."

"How about breakfast?" he asked. "Maybe we'll be fresher in the morning and we'll be able to come up with something we can all work with."

"John will go along with us, Clint," she said. "You can depend on him."

"And Mack?"

"Like I said," she replied, "he's out for himself. If there's glory in it, though, he'll go along."

"Well, then," Clint said, "we'll just have to try to make sure there's enough to go around while we're catching two killers."

"That'll work," she said. "Can I ask you something before you go?"

"Sure."

"Why are you doing this? I mean, you came here originally for a very different reason—probably to strangle me."

"Nothing like that," he said. "I just wanted to find out why you were tossing my name around."

"And now?"

"Now I just want to help, Darcy."

"But why?"

"Because I'm here," he said, "because I think you need it—you and your partners—and I think you have a better chance with me. Is that enough?"

"I guess—"

"Oh, yeah," he said, "one more thing."

"What's that?"

"I can't seem to manage to keep my nose out of other people's business."

She laughed and said, "I guess I'll accept all of those reasons. Good night."

"Good night."

They stood there awkwardly for a moment. If they had simply had dinner together he would have kissed her—hell, he would have accepted her invitation to come inside. Maybe she was feeling the attraction, too, but now wasn't the time to do anything about it.

Finally, she fitted her key into the lock and opened her door. He waited while she turned up the flame on the wall lamp.

"All right?"

"Yes," she said.

He was suddenly uncomfortable about letting her go in alone.

"Do you want me to check the bedroom?"

She thought a moment, then said, "Maybe you can wait while I check it."

"All right."

She took a small gun from her bag, put the bag down on a table, and walked to the other room. The gun was too small, and hidden by her body, for him to see anything but the fact that it was silver. When she returned to the door she was holding it down by her side.

"It's all right," she said, putting one hand on the door. "Thanks for waiting. I'll see you in the morning. Is nine o'clock all right?"

"That's fine," he said.

They said good night still again, and then she closed the door.

Clint waited until he heard the lock click, then walked down the hall, wondering what would have happened if he had accepted the invitation to come in.

THIRTY-ONE

"All right," Darcy said, "he's gone."

John Cable came out of the other room.

"Why'd you invite him in?"

She put her gun down on a table.

"Just being polite, I guess."

"You're not attracted to him, are you?"

"I find him very attractive, yes," she said. "Why?"

"He's too old for you."

"I see," she said. "Am I to get your opinion on the men I see, now?"

"No," he said, "that's not what I meant."

"And what are *you* doing in my room?"

"I wanted to talk."

"We had time to talk earlier."

"No," he said, "just you and me. We're partners, remember?"

"I'm tired, John," she said. "What do you want to talk about?"

"Our plans," he said. "We've got to decide what we're going to do."

"Clint and I talked about some ideas down in the dining room."

"I see," Cable said. "Is he calling the shots now?"

"Not at all," she said. "He's very willing to listen to ideas."

"That's great."

"We're going to have breakfast at nine," she said. "I suggest that you and Shane also come."

"Thanks for the invitation."

"Don't be sullen."

"I'm not."

"You are," she said. "You're pouting."

"I'm not!"

"Yes, you are. John, are you jealous?"

"No."

"Because if you are—"

"I'm not."

"If you are," she went on anyway, "it's not going to help."

"Don't worry, Darcy," he said, "I'll do my part."

"I know you will, John." She walked to him and put her hand on his arm. "I always know that."

"Yeah, well . . ." he said.

"Will you bring Shane and come to breakfast?" she asked. "We can all discuss ideas."

"We'll be there," he assured her.

"Good."

"Just remember, Darcy," he said, "*we're* the partners."

"I remember, John," she said. "Believe me, I wouldn't have it any other way."

"Well . . . all right, then."

"Good night."

"Night."

She walked Cable to the door and let him out. When she closed the door behind him, she leaned against it, shook her head, and said out loud, "Men are such children."

THIRTY-TWO

Cable heard Clint say he was going down to the bar so he went down there to find him. When he entered it was busy. There was no gambling in the hotel bar, but there were plenty of men there drinking to relax at the end of the day, and some women to help them do it. Cable stood just inside the door and studied the room until he found Clint sitting at a corner table with a beer.

He went to the bar, got himself a beer, and went to join him.

Clint saw John Cable the moment he entered. He waited patiently while the man located him, then got himself a beer and walked across the room to him.

"Cable," he said.

"Mind if I join you, Adams?"

"Have a seat."

Cable sat down.

"Since we're going to be working together you might as well call me Clint."

"I'm Cable," the man said, then grudgingly, "or John."

"I'll use Cable," Clint said. "What's on your mind?"

"Just wanted to talk."

"About what?"

"About Jason and Terry, what else?"

Clint shrugged.

"I thought you might want to talk about Darcy."

"What about her?"

"This Jason thing is an obsession with her."

"I know that."

"Can she think with a clear head about it?"

"Darcy's a professional," Cable said. "She'll do her job."

"Except that this isn't a job to her, is it?"

Cable hesitated, then said, "No, it isn't—but still, I trust her judgment."

Clint studied the man for a few moments, then nodded and said, "Okay, then, I'll accept your judgment and trust her, as well."

"Good."

"What about Mack?"

"What about him?"

"How's his judgment?"

"Mack's okay," Cable said. "Sometimes he'll rub you the wrong way, but he'll be there when we need him."

"Okay, good."

"You're accepting my word on all of this?" Cable asked.

"Sure, why not?" Clint asked. "Just as I'm accepting Darcy's word about you."

Cable remained silent.

"Don't you want to know what she said?"

"I know what she said," Cable replied. "We're partners,

remember? She said she could count on me.''

"That's right," Clint said. "You know each other real well, don't you?''

"Yeah, we do," Cable said. "We've been through a lot together.''

"And you probably love each other."

"What?"

"I said—"

"I heard you," Cable said. "Well, yeah, we love each other, but it's not—I mean, it's more like brother and—uh, well, it's just not what you think when you hear the word 'love.' ''

"I just meant as partners, and friends.''

"Oh, yeah, well, definitely, then. Yeah, we, uh, care about each other.''

"Then you'll help me keep her off the streets.''

"What?"

"She wants to go out on the street and make herself a target for Jason.''

"That's crazy.''

"That's about what I told her. I suggested we simply remain in the hotel and let him come to us. What do you think?''

"That makes sense," Cable agreed.

"Good," Clint said, "I'm glad we agree. Darcy and I are having breakfast at nine. Will you be there?''

"Yes," Cable said. "I already talked to her about it. I'll have Mack with me.''

"Good. We'll have to decide the best way to defend our position here. We want it to look like we're trying to keep him out, while what we're actually trying to do is entice him in.''

"Can the three of us do that?" Cable asked.

"I guess that's what we'll have to decide," Clint said. "We'll have to look around the hotel, locate all the entrances and exits.''

"All right.''

They had been working on their beers the whole time. Clint's was gone, and Cable lifted his to finish it.

"If you're up to it," Clint said, "I'd like to talk a little while longer."

"Sure, I'm up to it."

Clint stood up.

"I'll get two more beers, then. We should get to know each other a little better if we're going to be watching each other's backs."

Cable watched Clint walk to the bar and shook his head. Darcy had been right. He had been feeling jealous of Adams, but after talking to the man for ten minutes he found himself liking him.

Not trusting him yet, but liking him.

THIRTY-THREE

After about an hour and another beer, Cable leaned across the table and said, "Let me ask you something?"

"Go ahead."

"Why are you doing this?"

"Darcy asked me the same question."

"And what did you tell her?"

Clint decided to leave out the answer about him feeling that they needed him.

"I'm here, and I'm nosy."

"That's reason enough for you to risk your life?" Cable asked.

"I'm aware of something I wasn't aware of when I first got here."

"What's that?"

"That you and your partner are trying to do some good,"

Clint said. "You're trying to catch a couple of killers. That's enough reason for me. I hope it's enough for you to accept my help."

"Oh, I'll accept your help, all right," Cable said, "for the simple reason that I want this to be over for Darcy."

"I'll go along with that," Clint said, and they clinked beer mugs.

To anyone watching it would seem as if the two men were good friends, even though they'd only known each other a matter of hours.

"I have to tell you," Cable said, "I was pretty jealous of you before."

"Before what?" Clint asked.

"Before a few beers," Cable said, and they laughed. "No, I was kind of—well, I guess my ego was hurt, thinking that maybe we needed help, but with what happened to Selby and Blake and Wilson, I guess it's time to put ego aside."

"That's a good way to look at it, John," Clint said.

"Also—since I'm being honest—I guess I was jealous that Darcy was, you know, attracted to you."

"Darcy's a beautiful woman, John," Clint said, "but nothing has happened between us."

"I know, I know," Cable said. "I wish I could say it was different with us."

Clint remained silent, because he knew that Cable was now ready to talk and talk.

"I'd like something to happen between us," he said, "but she says not while we're partners. She says that would make it too hard to work together."

"She's probably right," Clint said.

"Yeah, I guess she is," Cable said. "Good partners are hard to find."

Clint could see from the look on the man's face and in his eyes, and hear from the way he was talking that he'd probably had enough to drink.

"Where are you staying?" Clint asked.

"A hotel down the street," Cable said, "a cheaper place."

"Come on," Clint said. "I'll walk over with you."

"I can make it—" Cable started to protest.

"I need the fresh air," Clint said. "Where is Mack?"

"He's at the same hotel," Cable said. "Look, you better stay here in case Darcy needs you. I'll get to my hotel okay."

"I think maybe tomorrow you and Mack should move to this hotel," Clint suggested. "It'll be better if we're all in one place."

"Sounds good," Cable said. "I'll see you at nine."

Clint walked out to the lobby with Cable and watched him go out the front door. He hoped that Lyle Jason and Earl Terry wouldn't pick tonight to make a move against Darcy, or either of the others.

They had one thing going for them as a team, and that was that Jason and Terry didn't know about Clint yet. Maybe they'd be able to keep it that way, and keep Clint as their ace in the hole.

Clint sat in the lobby for a while after Cable left, wondering if it was safe for him to go to his room and leave Darcy to her own devices for tonight.

He decided against it and went up to her room to check on her.

THIRTY-FOUR

Cable's hotel was actually two blocks away. When he got outside his head was buzzing, and as he walked he started to breathe deeply. It was probably silly to drink so much, and even sillier to start talking to Clint Adams the way he did. They'd probably work together for a couple of days or so, and then they'd never see each other again. What was the point of confiding in the man?

Cable was half a block from his hotel when he was suddenly hit from behind. The blow landed on his left shoulder and propelled him forward faster than he could handle. He stumbled and fell to the ground but had the presence of mind to roll as he hit. In doing so he avoided another, potentially more damaging blow which had been aimed at his head.

All he could think of was that he was being attacked by Lyle Jason or Earl Terry. As he rolled he reached into his jacket, grabbed his gun, and pulled it free of his shoulder holster.

Because he was in such excellent physical shape he managed to stop rolling, turn, and point his gun while in a crouch. The man who had hit him froze when he saw the gun, his hand over his head. In his hand he held what looked like a wooden club of some kind.

"Stop right there!" Cable shouted.

"Hey! Take it easy!" the man shouted. "Don't shoot. I just wanted your money, I wasn't really gonna hurt ya."

Tell that to my throbbing shoulder, Cable thought. The moon was full so he was able to see the man clearly. He was a thief, and maybe more, but he could see that it wasn't Lyle Jason or Earl Terry.

"You ain't gonna shoot, are ya?" the man asked.

"Drop that club."

The man did so immediately.

What Cable had to decide now was whether or not he wanted to send for the police and then stand around waiting for them. If he did that he'd end up having to go to the police station with them and press charges. By the time he got back it'd probably be time to meet Darcy and the others for breakfast. He decided against it. Besides, he didn't want any contact with the police at all.

"Mister?" the man asked. "You gonna shoot me?"

"No," Cable said, "I'm not going to shoot you."

He stood up but kept the gun trained on the man.

"Get out of here before I change my mind."

"I'm goin', mister. Thanks."

He bent to pick up the club, and Cable cocked the hammer on his gun.

"Leave it and go, now!"

The man turned and ran. Cable holstered his gun and

rubbed his shoulder. He hoped it wouldn't be stiff in the morning.

Stupid to drink so much, he thought, as he turned and headed for his hotel.

THIRTY-FIVE

When Darcy opened her door, Clint saw the surprise on her face. She was wearing a long dressing gown, holding it closed at the neck. He didn't know what she had on underneath. Her hair was tousled, as if she'd been lying down, but her eyes were bright and alert. He doubted that she had been asleep.

"Is something wrong?"

"No," he said, "I just spent the past couple of hours talking to your partner."

"John?" she said. "He came down and found you?"

He nodded.

"He didn't cause trouble, did he?"

"No, nothing like that," Clint said. "In fact, we had a pretty good talk."

"Oh? About what?"

"You, for one thing," he said. "Can I come in, instead of discussing it out in the hall?"

"I'm ready for bed."

"I want to ask you about something."

"All right."

She allowed him to enter and closed the door. When she turned to face him, she was no longer holding her gown together at the top. He could now see the tops of her firm breasts. He wondered if this was part of her high-class whore wardrobe.

"What's on your mind?" she asked him.

"You are."

"In what way?" she asked, eyeing him suspiciously.

"With Cable and Mack at their hotel for the night, I was worried about you."

She relaxed visibly.

"Oh. Well, do you think Jason would try something tonight? After all, he and Terry killed three men yesterday. Even he has to take a break."

"Chances are he'll want you to think about what he did for a while, but maybe I should stay here tonight, just in case."

"Here?" she asked. "Where?"

"Here," he said, waving a hand. "I can sleep on the sofa."

"Clint," she said, "I'm perfectly capable of taking care of myself, and I think we both agree that Jason's not going to try anything tonight."

"I guess you're right," he said.

"Have you been drinking?"

"John and I both were."

"John, is it?" she asked. "Have you two made friends?"

"I don't know if we're friends," Clint said, "but some of the tension is gone—I think. At least, I hope it will still be gone in the morning."

"John doesn't drink much, Clint," she said. "Was he all right to walk to his hotel?"

"I think he was fine. He *seemed* fine."

"What did you mean when you said you and he talked about me?"

"He has very strong feelings for you, Darcy."

"I care for him, too," she said, "but we're partners. He knows that as long as we are, nothing . . . romantic is going to happen."

"Yes, he told me that, too."

"I'm glad he did. I was afraid he was . . . jealous of you."

"Why would he need to be jealous of me?"

"Well . . . I mean, your reputation as . . . uh, well, the Gunsmith. You know . . . John likes to think he can handle anything that comes along without help. All men do."

"Really?" Clint asked. "Are you an expert on men?"

"I've known my share," she said. "Most of them are like children—and spoiled children, at that."

"I see."

"You may be different," she said, "I haven't had time to find out yet."

"Yet? You mean the time may come?"

"I just mean I don't know you very well, that's all," she said. "I don't know if we'll have time to change that."

"I don't know either," Clint said.

He was starting to have a hard time keeping his eyes off her cleavage, so he thought he'd better leave.

"Well, you know my room number," he said. "If you need anything, let me know."

"I will. Thanks for checking on me."

He walked to the door and opened it. She remained where she was, her arms at her sides. Her breasts were swelling with each breath, and he wondered why she was breathing so hard—or was he just drunk enough to think she was?

"Good night, Darcy."

"Good night, Clint . . . again."

He went out into the hall and closed the door, feeling

foolish. She probably thought that he had come back to try
to take her to bed. That wasn't the case at all. Not that he
wouldn't have wanted to. . . .

It made sense that Lyle Jason would want to give them
some time to think about what he'd done to their partners.
That kind of man usually perpetrated his violence and then
allowed it to play on the minds of others.

Nailing a man to the wall, that was done for shock value
and little else. From what Clint had heard while eavesdropping, the others had been pretty damned shocked.

He found it pretty shocking, himself.

THIRTY-SIX

Earl Terry was lying on the bed when the door to the room opened and Lyle Jason walked in. Terry was surprised that Jason had a girl with him, a big dark-haired girl with big hips and breasts.

"Earl," Jason said as he came in, "go find something to do."

"Like what?" Terry asked, bringing his feet off the bed and pulling on his boots. Jason rarely had to tell the big man anything twice.

"I don't care," Jason said. He pulled the girl to him and pawed her breasts. She laughed and pulled the top of her dress down so her naked breasts popped free. They were big, pear-shaped things with chocolate nipples. Terry thought she was too big for Jason. She was more his size.

"Come on, Earl," Jason said. He grabbed the big man's elbow and walked him to the door.

"Lyle?" Terry asked as Jason pushed him into the hall.

"What?"

"You ain't gonna kill her, are you?"

"No," Jason said, "I'm just gonna use her, Earl. The girl I'm going to kill is over at the Denver House hotel, remember?"

"I remember, Lyle," Terry said, "but when are we gonna do it and leave?"

"There's no hurry, Earl," Jason said. "Let's give them time to think about what happened to their friends, huh?"

"Yeah," Terry said, "but—"

"Look," Jason said, "come back in about an hour, huh? By then I should be done and you can have this whore if you want her. She's a big girl, ain't she?"

She was a big girl and suddenly Earl Terry didn't think that would be such a bad idea.

"Okay, Lyle," he said. "I'll be back in an hour."

"Good," Jason said, and closed the door with a slam, leaving Terry standing in the hall.

Terry wasn't sure what to do and stood there for a few moments. He heard the girl inside laugh and then moan. The hotel was not a big one, but it did have a saloon in it. He decided to spend the hour down there.

He just hoped Jason wouldn't kill the girl. After all, it had been a while.

After Lyle Jason closed the door in Earl Terry's face, he turned to look at the girl. She had taken off all her clothes and was standing there waiting for him.

"Where'd your friend go?" she asked. "Don't he want to play?"

"You interested in my friend?"

"He's a big man."

"Yeah, well, maybe I'll let you play with him later. Right now you gotta play with me."

"Well, I'm ready," she said. Her right hand was down between her legs, disappearing into the bushiest pussy Lyle Jason had ever seen. "Come and get it, lover. It's all wet and waitin' for you."

THIRTY-SEVEN

Clint had taken off his boots and shirt and was washing up in a basin of water when there was a knock on his door. He frowned, dried his hands on a towel, drew his gun from his holster, which was hanging on the bedpost, and then walked to the door.

"Who is it?"

"It's Darcy."

He opened the door quickly.

"Is something wrong?"

She was standing in the hall, holding herself, as if she was cold. She had gotten dressed in a shirt, Levi's, and boots.

"Can I come in?"

"Sure, of course."

She entered and he closed the door.

"It's a little smaller than your room," he said.

"It's fine," she said. "Mine's too big . . . in fact, that's why I'm here."

"Why?"

"Because my room is too big," she said again. "I know it sounds silly but . . . I keep thinking somebody's trying to get in, you know? The front door, the window. I keep thinking, what if Jason is figuring that we'll figure that he wants to give us time to think? What if he does try to get to me tonight? I keep thinking—"

"You're thinking too much," Clint said, cutting her off, "that's your problem."

"I know."

"Do you want to spend the night here, Darcy?"

She was still standing as if she were cold, looking down at her feet, and she nodded.

"I don't have a sofa to sleep on," he said.

"That's all right," she said, looking at him now. "That's something else I've been thinking about."

"What?"

"You," she said, "me, a bed . . . that bed."

"Darcy . . . are you sure?"

"If you don't mind the reason."

"And what is the reason?"

"I might be dead tomorrow," she said. "Or the next day."

"I don't think—"

"I'm saying there's a possibility."

"Okay," he agreed, "there is a possibility."

She stopped clutching herself and moved closer to him. She put her hands on his bare chest, and they *were* cold.

"I want to be with someone tonight, Clint."

"What about Cable?"

She shook her head.

"I want to be with you. I want to feel your arms around me, I want to feel your mouth on me, I want you *inside* me. I want to feel alive!"

She leaned forward and kissed his chest, circling one of his nipples with her tongue.

He reached behind her head, took hold of her hair, pulled her head back and kissed her. Her mouth was cold but sweet, and her tongue pushed past his lips into his mouth.

Her nails raked his back while they kissed. He pulled her shirt from her pants and then, without unbuttoning it, just pulled it over her head. She was naked underneath. Her breasts, mashed against his chest, were hot.

Her mouth had warmed up and her kisses were avid, almost desperate. They undid each other's belts and he helped her with her boots, and then they stripped off each other's trousers and were naked together.

"Come to bed," he said, putting his arm around her, "I'll warm you."

They went to his bed and got in together. Under the covers they pressed their bodies together and kissed again. Their legs entwined and she reached between them to touch his turgid penis. He slid his hands behind her to cup her butt, which was cool, but warming up.

Her behind was firm and smooth, her breasts also firm against his chest, the nipples as hard as pebbles. He put one hand between them, slid it down over her belly until it was between her legs, where she was slick and wet.

"I can't wait," she said in his ear, "I want you inside me."

"I want to go slow," he said.

"Go slow later!" she said urgently.

She was frantic for him so he decided not to make her wait. She rolled onto her back, pulling at him. He mounted her and drove himself into her, and she gasped and clutched him to her.

She wrapped her legs up around him and he slid his hands beneath her to cup her ass. Every time he drove into her he pulled her to him. She grunted, lifting her hips to meet each of his thrusts, and they did that for what seemed a very long time. Finally Clint drew himself upright, but did not slide away from her. Instead he grabbed her ankles and lifted her legs up, spread them, and continued to bang into her that way.

Later still she pushed away from him only to roll onto her belly and then get to her knees. Clint obliged her by pressing himself against her butt and entering her from behind. She grasped the bedpost in both hands and grunted loudly every time he slammed his pelvis against her butt.

"Yes, yes, yes," she chanted, driving her ass back against him, taking him up inside of her hard until finally Clint couldn't hold it in anymore. He exploded into her, shouting as he did so, aware that she was also yelling, and to hell with anyone in the hotel who didn't like it . . .

THIRTY-EIGHT

When Earl Terry returned to the hotel room he was happy to find the whore still alive. He was also happy that Lyle Jason seemed pleased with her.

"There you are," Jason said as he entered. "This is Michelle, and she's been waiting for you."

"Waiting for me?"

Jason raised his eyebrows and said, "She likes big men."

Jason got out of bed, completely naked, and dressed quickly.

"She's all yours, partner," he said, surprising Terry with his apparent good spirits and his willingness to share a woman.

"Where are you going?" Terry asked.

"For a walk," Jason said. "I think I'm getting tired of Denver."

"We're gonna leave?" Terry asked anxiously.

"Sure we are, Earl," Jason said, "as soon as I remove a little thorn from my side—if you know what I mean."

"Huh?"

Jason smiled and walked past Terry to the door.

"Never mind," he said, opening the door. "Just have a good time with Michelle, and I'll be back in a couple of hours."

"A couple of hours—" Terry said, but Jason was gone.

The big man turned to look at the naked woman, who had moved from Jason's bed to his.

"I love fresh sheets," she said, rubbing her hand over them.

Earl Terry couldn't take his eyes off of her. She was on all fours, running her hands over the sheets—which had been changed that morning—and her pear-shaped breasts were hanging down and swaying, the nipples fully distended.

No wonder she liked big men, he thought, she was a big woman.

"I can see from here that you're interested in me," she said.

Terry looked down and saw that his erection was obvious, even through his pants. He couldn't remember ever having one this big before. Usually he was interested in sex a few times a month. His lack of interest stemmed from the fact that he didn't think he was very good at it. Right now, though, he couldn't recall ever having been this excited. He was even afraid to move for fear of making a mess before he could get undressed.

There was something different about this woman. She was up on her knees on the bed now, smiling at him and fingering herself, and he could *smell* her!

"Are you ready for me, big man?" she asked. "Or do I have to come over there and get you?"

"I—I—"

"Are you nervous?"

"Y-yes," he admitted.

"How sweet."

Suddenly, she abandoned the lascivious pose she'd been affecting. She got off the bed and walked to where he was standing.

"You don't have to be nervous, lover," she said, taking his hand. "Just leave everything to Michelle, okay?"

"O-okay."

She loosened his belt and unbuttoned his pants, and he couldn't believe how gentle she was.

She tugged his pants and shorts down to his ankles and his erection popped free, huge and pulsing.

"There you are. Ooh, I just knew you'd be that big."

Terry stared down at himself. How could she have known he'd be that big when *he* didn't know it?

"Just relax, baby," she said, getting on her knees in front of him.

God, if she touched him now . . .

"Don't worry," she said, as if reading his mind. She took hold of him at the base of his penis, wrapping one hand around him and squeezing tightly. Suddenly, the urge to ejaculate was not as strong.

"Nothing will happen until I want it to," she told him, looking up at him. "Not until I make it, understand?"

"Yes?"

"Don't be nervous, and don't worry," she said, eyeing his swollen penis. "We're gonna have a good time." She kissed the tip of his penis, then ran her tongue around it, making him moan.

"A really *good* time," she said.

THIRTY-NINE

Later they made love more gently, slowly, making it last. They were belly to belly this time when he emptied into her and she clutched him to her, biting him on the shoulder. . . .

"I left a mark," she said, still later. She kissed the spot where she had bitten his shoulder too hard.

"That's okay."

They were lying together on the bed, she spooned up against his back.

"I should have asked this before," she said, her mouth against his back, "but is there a wife or a girlfriend somewhere?"

"No wife," he said, thinking about Anne Archer, the

lady bounty hunter who was the closest thing to a woman in his life for more than an evening.

"A girlfriend?"

"Lots of women who are friends," he said.

"Okay," she said, "I'll stop asking questions."

"No men in D.C.?" he asked. "Suitors?"

"Always," she said. "In Washington there are always interested men, there just aren't always interesting men."

"I see."

"Besides," she said, pressing her cheek to his back this time, "I guess I haven't been very interested in men since . . . since my sister was killed."

"Maybe once this is over you should give it some thought," Clint said.

"Once this is over?"

"When Jason is taken care of."

"When that happens I'll go back to work for the Service," she said. "I've got a career to think of."

"In the Secret Service?"

"Why not?"

"There must be something else you want to do, Darcy."

"You mean like get married, have children, raise a family?"

"Maybe."

"Maybe not," she said. "That's not really something I'm interested in, Clint."

"Nobody says you have to be." Her arms were around his waist. He rubbed them and said, "We better get some sleep."

"Okay," she said, "I'll go to sleep . . . for a while."

"A while?"

She slid one hand down his body and said, "Just until you get your breath back."

She touched him and felt him respond.

"Hmm," she said, "maybe you already have."

"That's just my body," he said, "betraying me. Ignore it and go to sleep."

She didn't ignore it and when she finally fell asleep she was still holding him in her hand.

FORTY

When Lyle Jason returned to the room he shared with Earl Terry, the big man was asleep. He could tell by the way he was breathing. Jason was surprised to see that Michelle, the whore, was also asleep, draped over Terry's big body.

Jason didn't understand it, but Earl Terry was virtually the only man he had ever liked. He got the impression, from the way the two of them were sleeping, that they'd had a real good time, and he was glad of that.

He knew that Terry didn't like Denver. That was part of the reason he'd gone out tonight to scout the Denver House hotel. He wanted to check all of the exits and entrances, because tomorrow night he and Terry were going to go in and get rid of the woman who had been hunting him for most of the year.

He got undressed and got into bed. The sheets still smelled of the woman, but that was okay with him. There was a moment while he was having sex with her when he found his hands around her neck. It would have been very easy to strangle her, even though she was a large woman. He didn't do it for two reasons. He was already planning to kill a "whore" tomorrow, and killing this one now would just be too dangerous.

The second reason was Earl Terry. He thought the woman would be good for his partner, and it looked as though he'd been right. He had never seen Terry sleep with a woman before.

He pulled the sheet and blanket up over his shoulders and turned his back on the two sleeping lovebirds. His mind went back to the business at hand.

In the beginning, when Jason had first realized that he was being hunted by a woman, he'd thought it was funny. Months later, though, when she was still looking for him it wasn't that funny anymore. Now that he realized that she'd had *five* men here in Denver with her to try to catch him he knew he had to get rid of her.

What he still didn't know was why this woman was after him. He hoped that, tomorrow night, before he killed her, she would tell him.

FORTY-ONE

When Clint and Darcy came down for breakfast, both John Cable and Shane Mack were already there. Clint hoped that the men wouldn't be able to tell by looking at them that they had spent the night in the same bed. They really didn't need the extra complications this might cause, specifically with Cable.

"Good morning," Darcy greeted. Cable stood up as she arrived, but Mack did not. Her partner helped her with her chair.

"Morning," Clint said.

"What happened to you?" Darcy asked Cable.

She must have had a very good eye, probably as a result of having been partners with him, because Clint couldn't see anything wrong with him.

"My shoulder is stiff," Cable said, sitting.

"Why?"

"He got attacked last night," Mack said.

"Was it Jason?" Darcy asked. "Are you all right?"

"I'm fine," Cable said. "When it happened I thought it might be Jason, or Earl Terry, but it wasn't. It was just some thief after my money."

"How badly are you hurt?" Clint asked.

"He hit me with some kind of club," Cable said. "It caught me on the shoulder. It's not bad, just stiff, as if I'd slept on it or something. It'll work itself out." He looked at Darcy. "Don't worry about it."

"All right," she said.

Clint wondered if Cable could tell just by looking at Darcy that something had happened last night, as she had been able to tell by looking at him. Probably not, since what happened to Cable was a physical injury, and what happened between him and Darcy, while physical, was certainly not an injury.

"Have you ordered breakfast?" Darcy asked.

"Cable wanted to wait for you," Mack said. It was obvious that he was hungry.

"Well, let's do it, then," she said, "and then we can talk."

They called a waiter over and ordered breakfast. The three men ordered full breakfasts of eggs and bacon and grits and biscuits, while Darcy said she'd just have biscuits and asked the waiter if he had marmalade. Clint told the waiter to bring some coffee quickly.

"I understand you and Clint had a talk last night," Darcy said.

"I heard about that, too," Mack said. "Anything interesting come out of it?"

"We sort of decided that we should wait for Jason to make a move before doing anything," Cable said.

"Like his last move?" Mack asked. "Three of us are dead. I think we should go looking for him."

"Fine," Darcy said, "where would you suggest we look first?"

Mack opened his mouth to answer, then closed it.

"Exactly," Clint said. "I think we only have two options."

"Waiting for him is the first," Cable said, "what's the second?"

"Giving up and going home."

"No," Darcy said, "that's out. I have a third option."

"What's that?" Mack asked.

"I'm the target," she said. "I'm the one that's been after him for months. I think I should go outside and give him a chance to get to me."

"And then we grab him," Mack said, "either before he can kill you . . . or after he does."

"No," Cable said, "that's out."

"That's what I said," Clint agreed.

"We can't protect you outside, Darcy," Cable said.

"But who knows when he'll make a move?" she asked. "We could be waiting days, maybe weeks."

"Not weeks," Cable said. "I don't think he'll stay in one place that long. And remember, he likes killing whores. I think he lives for that. He couldn't go that long without killing one."

Mack looked at Darcy and said, "I guess if he's after Darcy he thinks of her as his next whore."

Clint could see that the remark upset Cable, and he didn't know Mack well enough to know if that was his intention, but the remark did make sense.

"If that is the case," Clint said, "then I don't think we'll have that long to wait. Maybe a matter of days."

"Or hours," Mack said.

The coffee came first and the waiter poured out four cups, and then the food followed shortly after. They continued to talk while they ate.

"I think we have to find the two points in the hotel where he'd be most likely to try to get in," Clint said.

"Two?" Mack asked. "There are three of us."

"I think one of us should stay with Darcy at all times."

"Now wait a minute," Darcy said. "I have a gun and I know how to use it, and don't forget that I'm every bit as much a Secret Service agent as Cable and Mack. I don't need someone to hold my hand."

At that point she gave Clint a look, obviously thinking about what had happened last night. Clint saw it, and wondered if either of the other men saw it, as well.

"All right," Cable said, "then we need to find the three most likely points of entry and cover them."

"We can't do that for twenty-four hours," Mack said.

"That's true," Clint said.

"What do we do then?" Darcy asked.

The three Secret Service agents looked at Clint, who was the most experienced of the four.

"We'll just have to make an educated guess as to what time of day he'll make his move."

"And if we guess wrong?" Cable asked.

Nobody seemed to want to answer that question.

FORTY-TWO

They continued to discuss it over breakfast, and more coffee.

"Daytime," Mack said.

"Nightime," Cable said.

"Two and two," Clint said.

The other three looked at him and Darcy asked, "What?"

"We should work in shifts of two and two," Clint said, "that way we can cover things day and night."

"What happened to covering the exits?" Mack asked.

Clint shrugged.

"Can't do it, unless we can bring in more people."

"We can't do that," Darcy said.

"Why not the police?" Clint asked.

"They'd ask questions," Cable said, "and we can't answer questions."

"We're not allowed to," Mack explained.

"Then we'll have to make do."

"And how do we do that?" Cable asked.

"Easy," Clint said. "We stop worrying about how he's going to get into the hotel."

"And do what instead?" Mack asked.

"Cover the hall outside of Darcy's room," Clint said. "He's got to come down that hall to get to her."

"We'll need another room," Cable said. "We can't just sit out in the hall."

"I think Darcy can take care of that for us," Clint said. "She'll just have to talk to Mr. Roulet, the hotel manager."

Darcy smiled.

"I can do that."

"Now the question of how we pair up," Mack said.

"That's easy," Cable said. "Me and Darcy, since we're partners."

Darcy looked at Clint, who tried to warn her off with a look.

"That sounds fine to me," Clint said. "Okay with you, Mack?"

"Sure, fine," Mack said. "Anything to get this over with. Maybe I'll even learn something."

Because of that remark—apparently spoken sincerely—Clint thought there might be more to Shane Mack than was readily apparent.

After breakfast was over it was decided that Darcy and Clint would go and talk to Roulet. Cable and Mack would go to their hotel, get their belongings, and move into the extra room.

They split up in the lobby and agreed to meet in Darcy's room in an hour.

FORTY-THREE

"B-but that's a suite," Roulet said when they went to his office with their request.

"But, Pierre," Darcy said, coming around to his side of the desk and perching on the end of it, "we really need it. Please?" She played with his tie. "For me?"

Roulet frowned, knowing he was outclassed again, and asked, "For how long?"

Once they had secured the other room, they moved Cable and Mack in. It was almost directly across from Darcy's, with the added advantage that Jason would have to pass their door before he reached hers.

"What about the windows?" Mack asked. "Is there access from outside?"

"Not simple access," Clint said. "Somebody would

have to come down from the roof, and there's no ledge outside.''

"Who's going to take the first watch?" Cable asked.

"I think there should be a change in the pairing," Darcy said.

"Why?" Cable asked.

"Because you and Mack are sharing the room," she said. "You fellas should pair up. You can both sleep at the same time that way."

Cable frowned, not liking it.

"Mack?" Darcy asked. "Do you mind?"

"I don't mind."

"Clint?"

"It's okay with me if it's okay with Cable," he said, hoping that deferring to Cable's decision would soften the blow for the man.

"I guess so," Cable finally said. "It makes sense."

"Sure, it does," Darcy said, and turning her back to Cable and Mack she gave Clint a knowing smile.

"That was slick," Clint said, when they were in her room, "and a little mean."

"I've got another idea," she said, coming into his arms.

"What's that?"

"I think you should move your things in here."

"Now that's not such a good idea."

"Why not?"

"What do you think your partner would say to that?"

"We'll tell him that you're going to sleep on the sofa."

"It won't work."

"Why not?"

"You already know that he's jealous, Darcy," Clint said, "why do you want to make it worse?"

She hesitated a moment, then said, "I suppose you're right."

"Sure I am."

She kissed him then, soundly enough to make his legs

weak, and said, "Then come to bed now, Mr. Adams. If I have to be without you at night you're going to have to make it up to me in the daytime."

"They're sleeping together," Mack said, after Clint and Darcy left their room.

"What?" Cable asked.

"They're sleeping together," Mack said again.

"You're crazy."

"You can't see it?"

"There's nothing to see."

"I can see it," Mack said, "I don't know why you can't."

"Because there's nothing to see."

"You can tell by the way she looks at him."

"What makes you such an authority on women?" Cable demanded.

"You don't have to be an authority, Cable," Mack said, "all you have to do is open your eyes."

Cable didn't want to open his eyes—not to that.

"They're not sleeping together."

"Suit yourself," Mack said. "Which room do you want?"

FORTY-FOUR

In the morning when Terry woke up, he was surprised Michelle wasn't there. He rolled over and took a quick look at Jason's bed, hoping she wouldn't be there. He breathed a sigh of relief when he saw that his partner was alone in his bed, and still asleep.

Earl Terry couldn't believe what had happened last night. He had never had a night like that with a woman in his life, and suddenly Denver didn't seem so bad—not if there were more nights like that ahead of him.

He swung his feet to the floor and sat like that for a few minutes, replaying some of the night's moments in his head. While he was doing that Lyle Jason woke up.

"What are you doing?" he asked.

"Where'd she go?" Terry asked. "Why did she leave without waking me up?"

163

Jason took one look at his partner and knew they were in trouble. The big fool had gone and fallen for a whore.

"She's a whore, Earl," he said.

"So?"

"I paid her for the night. Now it's morning, and she's gone."

"What are you saying?" Terry asked.

"She's gone, that's all I'm saying."

"But she'll come back, right?"

"Oh, sure," Jason said, "if you pay her."

Terry thought a moment and then said, "I got money."

"Don't worry about it," Jason said, swinging his legs to the floor so he was sitting directly opposite Terry.

"Whataya mean?"

"We won't be here that long."

"W-what?"

"I'm going to take care of the girl tonight, and then we're leaving Denver."

Terry thought about that a moment and didn't like it at all.

"Well . . . I don't wanna leave Denver." He whined it, like a child.

"You've been nagging me to leave since we got here!"

"That was before Michelle."

"Oh, Earl . . ."

"What's the matter?"

"You fell in love with a whore, Earl."

"She's nice."

"She'll be nice to any man who pays her, Earl," Jason said. "Forget about her."

"I can pay her."

"And what will you do when you run out of money?"

"Get more."

"Look, Earl," Jason said, tapping the man on his knee, "I'm leaving Denver tomorrow. Are you going to stay here alone?"

"I don't want to be alone, Lyle."

"Then you'll be coming with me."

"Why don't we stay here?"

"Earl," Jason said, "I'll get you another whore."

"She won't be like Michelle."

"She'll be exactly like Michelle," Jason said. "She'll let you touch her, she'll touch you, she'll let you—"

"Will she be nice?"

"She'll be as nice as you want her to be."

"Where is she?"

"She's in Dodge City . . ."

"Oh."

". . . and Tucson, and Taos, and Springfield, and Flagstaff, there's one in every town, Earl."

"Oh."

"Can we stop talking about this now?" Jason asked.

"Sure, Lyle," Terry said glumly.

"I walked over to the Denver House hotel last night, and I know how we're going to get in—are you listening to me?"

"I'm listening."

"You better get this straight, because there are still some men you're going to have to take care of while I handle the woman."

"Okay, Lyle," Terry said, "I'll get it straight."

While Jason talked, Earl Terry realized he was feeling something for Lyle Jason that he had never felt before. He couldn't put his finger on it at first, but then it came to him. It was an emotion he had never felt for Jason before.

Annoyance.

FORTY-FIVE

Instead of staying in Darcy's room, which he knew would cause some friction between him and Cable—and maybe Darcy and Cable—Clint went across the hall and stayed in the other room. He moved a chair to the door, left the door open a crack, and sat.

Cable and Mack were supposed to be trying to get some sleep, since they would have the night shift. For this reason Clint was surprised when Cable came up behind him.

"I hate this part."

"The waiting?" Clint asked.

Cable nodded.

"I don't have the patience for it," he said to Clint. "I'm more comfortable with the action."

"You learn patience over the years," Clint said. "Aren't you supposed to be sleeping?"

"I can't sleep during the day."

"Then you and Mack should have taken the day and I would have taken the night with Darcy."

"Mack is sleeping like a baby," Cable said. "It doesn't matter, really. I don't usually sleep that much, anyway."

Clint sat up straight, stretching his back. It had only been a few hours, but he was falling into the habit of sitting hunched over, and his back was getting stiff. He could sit in the saddle with no difficulty longer than he could do this.

"Want me to spell you?" Cable asked.

"I don't think—"

"I might as well, since I'm here."

Clint thought standing and walking around a bit might help him.

"All right."

They changed places and Clint stretched again, this time while standing. It felt good. He walked over to the window and looked outside. The street below was busy. Lyle Jason would be able to blend in very easily, but from the description he'd heard of Earl Terry the big man would stand out.

"How are they going to do it, I wonder?" he said out loud.

"Do what?"

Clint turned from the window and looked at Cable's back. The man had already adopted his hunched over approach to sitting there.

"I was just wondering how Jason expects to get into the hotel. He's got to know that you and Mack are still around."

"Maybe he figures it will be easy, since he's already killed three of us."

"But that was different. Two of the men he killed were in an abandoned building, and the third was on the street. The rest of you are holed up in a big hotel."

"Well, a hotel is full of people," Cable said. "They could blend in as guests."

"Jason could," Clint said, "but you told me Earl Terry was a big man. He couldn't blend in so easily."

"That's true."

Clint was thinking quickly now.

"A diversion," he said, "they'd need some kind of diversion."

"Like what?" Cable asked. But before Clint could answer Cable sniffed the air and asked, "Do you smell smoke?"

Earl Terry did just like Jason told him to do. He found the back door of the hotel, the one that led to the kitchen, and he waited. Sooner or later, Jason told him, somebody had to come out to throw away some garbage. When that happened Terry was supposed to use whatever means necessary to get through that door. Terry didn't know why Jason had suddenly decided to make his move during the day instead of at night. One minute they were talking about Michelle, and the next Jason was telling him to get dressed, that they were going to go do it right now.

Terry didn't like the way Jason talked about Michelle. Sure she was a whore and did what she did for money, Terry knew that. He wasn't stupid. But he also knew that she'd been real nice to him, and that counted for more than anything. Other than Jason, she was the only person to be nice to him—although "nice" wasn't really a word he'd use when thinking about Jason. The other man took care of him, and told him what to do, which he appreciated. When he had to try to decide what to do on his own it always gave him such a headache.

Take now, for instance. He knew that he had to stand here and wait for that door to open. That was easy. He didn't care how long it took, he'd wait, and then he'd do what Jason told him to do.

He'd been standing there three hours when the door finally opened. A man stepped out carrying a box that was filled with trash. The man walked to a bigger receptacle, and as he was about to throw the box inside Terry came up behind him and broke his neck. He then threw the box and the man into the large receptacle.

Terry walked to the door, hoping he hadn't made a mistake. Maybe he should have waited for the man to open the door again. What if it had locked behind him? He tried the doorknob and was relieved to find that it turned, and the door opened.

He was inside the hotel. Now he had to find a likely place for a fire.

Darcy sat up straight in her chair and sniffed the air. She wasn't sure, but she thought she smelled smoke. She went to the door and opened it, and saw Cable and Clint standing in the doorway across the hall.

"Are you thinking what I'm thinking?" she asked.

"Yes," Clint said. "We were just talking about a diversion."

"This might be it," Cable said. "I better wake Mack."

"Darcy, why don't you come over here," Clint said.

"Let me get my gun."

She went back into the room to get her gun, closing the door behind her.

At that point Cable came out of the other bedroom with Mack, who was stumbling.

"Maybe you two better go downstairs and see if we're overreacting," Clint said. "Darcy and I will hold the fort here."

"They're probably burning somebody's lunch in the kitchen or something," Mack complained, strapping on his gun.

"Well, we'll just go and find out," Cable said. He looked at Clint. "Be right back."

Clint nodded. Cable and Mack went out into the hall and headed for the stairs.

Clint looked across the hall at Darcy's door and wondered what was taking so long.

FORTY-SIX

Darcy looked around and swore that she'd left her gun on the table near the door. She decided maybe she had left it in the bedroom, and when she went in there she saw it. Unfortunately it was being held by a man.

"Hello, Darcy."

"Jason."

"Close the door."

She knew if she closed the door she was finished. There was no way Clint and Cable and Mack would hear her through two closed doors.

"Let's go in the other room," she said.

"No," he said, "I like it in this room. Close the door."

Reluctantly she closed the door and then turned to face him.

"My partners are right across the hall."

"They'll be occupied by the fire," Jason said. "I wouldn't want them to disturb us."

"How did you get in here?"

"The window."

She looked at it and saw that it was open.

"There's no ledge."

"Oh, there's a very small one," Jason said, "enough for my toes. All I needed to do was come down from the roof on a rope."

"How did you get to the roof?"

"That was easy," he said. "I walked in the front door, took a room, requested one on this very floor, all the way at the other end. Did you know that there's access to the roof from both this end of the floor and my end? There's a hatch in the ceiling in the hall. I just went up, over to the other side, and down a rope that they use to wash the windows. It was easy."

Darcy couldn't believe it. That was much more than they expected him to do.

"Impressed?"

"Yes."

"That's good," he said. "I want you to be impressed with me. I'm very impressed with you."

"Are you?"

"Oh, yes," he said. "You're very beautiful, but you're also very persistent. You've been after me for months now. You've taken it to the point I have to do something about it."

"Do it, then."

"In due time," he said. "There's no rush. Tell me, why are you after me so relentlessly?"

"You killed my sister."

"I did? Oh, you mean one of those nameless, faceless whores I killed was your sister?"

"Yes."

"Too bad." There was no remorse whatsoever.

"You bastard."

"I'll tell you what," he said. "I don't remember your sister, but I'll bet she enjoyed her last moments—just like you're going to."

"You bastard!" she said again, and took a step forward.

"Go ahead," he said, "make me do it now."

Darcy stopped. The longer she was alive the more chance she had to stop him.

"That's a smart girl," Jason said. "We're going to get better acquainted. Take off your clothes."

"What?"

"Get undressed."

She glared at him.

"Do it, Darcy."

"I'll do it," she said, "but don't say my name."

"Fine."

While he watched she undressed, and when she was naked he shook his head.

"God, you're beautiful."

He was so obviously impressed by her beauty that she was starting to wonder if she could use it against him.

FORTY-SEVEN

Cable and Mack reached the lobby and saw that people were moving about in a frenzy, with smoke filling the air. The clerk behind the desk was shouting to them to keep calm, that everything was under control.

The two men ran to the front desk and asked the clerk what was going on.

"We had a small fire in the kitchen," he said, "mostly smoke."

"Is it under control?"

"Yes," the man said, "but these people won't believe me. You can see most of the smoke is up near the ceiling now. There's no danger."

"Where's the manager?"

"In the kitchen."

They went through the dining room and saw the smoke

coming from a doorway. They ran to it and entered the kitchen.

"Jesus," Cable said.

"God," Mack said.

The floor was strewn with bodies, most of the white-clad kitchen staff, but one of them was wearing a dark suit. Cable recognized him as the manager, Pierre Roulet.

"Are they dead?" Mack asked.

"Some of them," Cable said. "Look at their heads."

There were at least two men whose heads were at odd angles, indicating broken necks.

"We better get back to Darcy," Cable said. "Something's happening now."

Before they could move, something slammed into their backs and sent them staggering forward. Cable had a quick flash of how foolish they had been to stand so close together. When they fell to the floor their guns went skittering across the floor.

Cable turned around to look up at their attacker. The man was massive, and there was no mistaking it was Earl Terry.

Terry watched as the two men entered the kitchen with their guns out. He recognized one of them from when he and Jason were watching the hotel. He came up behind them while they were looking around and stiff-armed them both, driving the heel of his hand into their backs. They looked comical staggering forward and falling to the floor, then sliding as they lost their guns. He watched as one of the guns slid underneath a counter. He didn't see where the other one went. Once they were disarmed he was confident he could handle them.

He wondered how Jason was doing.

Lyle Jason held the gun in one hand and with the other cupped one of Darcy's breasts.

"Mmm, beautiful," he said, squeezing it, "and firm."

Darcy closed her eyes as he touched her, and tried to keep from shuddering.

"Why don't we move to the bed?" she asked.

He laughed and squeezed her breast harder. She bit her lip to keep from crying out in pain.

"Little whore," he said. "Think you can entice me into bed and handle me there, don't you?"

"I just thought—"

"You just stand there, little whore," he said, sliding the hand down her body, over her belly and between her legs, making her jump. He said, "Just relax and enjoy it."

Cable looked around but couldn't find his gun. He started looking around for something else to use as a weapon. Mack, on the other hand, bounded to his feet and charged the big man. Cable was torn between watching the two men clash and finding something, anything, that he could use. It was a kitchen, after all, there had to be something sharp. . . .

Cable heard a loud crack and quickly looked back at Terry and Mack. The big man was holding Shane Mack in his hands like a rag doll, and Mack's head was tilted at an impossible angle.

Jesus, it was that easy to kill him?

Cable got to his feet as Earl Terry tossed Mack away as if he were weightless. The body landed on a counter and utensils went flying. Cable watched as a knife hit the floor, and he fixated on it.

Terry moved forward, his arms wide. From fingertip to fingertip the span was amazing. Cable had to get by him to get to the knife. Terry's stance was wide, so Cable charged him and went in lower than Mack had done. Terry's arms closed above him. The floor was slippery and Cable slid right between Terry's legs. He struck a blow as he did so, trying to hit him in the balls. He missed and the blow was ineffectual, but at last he was behind the man.

He got to his feet quickly and kicked out before Terry

could turn. His heel struck the back of Terry's knee, making it buckle. Terry cried out, so Cable knew he had hurt him. As the big man was off balance he punched him in the back of the neck and then kicked him in the ass. The man was off balance, and Cable saw his chance.

He turned and looked down and immediately spotted the knife. He grabbed it and turned back. Terry had one hand on the floor and was pushing himself back to a standing position. Cable jumped in and kicked the back of the other knee. Terry cried out, and with both knees damaged he fell to one of them, reaching his hand out to the floor again.

Cable moved quickly. He grabbed Terry by the hair, yanked his head way back, exposing his throat. He whipped the knife across the man's neck, hoping it was sharp enough, and it was. In fact, it was razor-sharp. He sliced the big man open from ear to ear and blood poured out onto his shirt. Incredibly, Terry swept an arm back and struck Cable a blow that sent him staggering. He watched as the man regained his feet and turned to face him. His eyes were wild, and blood was pouring down his chest. There was a puzzled look on his face, and as he opened his mouth to speak nothing intelligible came out.

"Die, damn you!" Cable shouted.

Earl Terry knew he was going to die. He opened his mouth to speak but couldn't. He wanted to say Michelle's name, and he didn't know why. Why was he thinking of her at the moment of his death?

Why not?

What else was there about his life that was pleasant enough to recall at that moment?

Lyle Jason began to rub his left hand over her pubic mound. His right hand held the gun, but he did not have it pressed against her. This invasion of her body was obscene, and she finally couldn't stand it anymore.

"No!" she shouted, and struck out at him.

She punched him in the face and pushed him away from her. He staggered back.

"No more," she said.

He backed up only a few steps, then looked at her and smiled.

"You know what?" he said. "I think I'll play with you after. That's probably what I did to your sister."

She growled like an animal and threw herself at him, waiting for the sound of the shot and the burn of the bullet as it ripped through her body. She heard the shot, but didn't feel anything. Could a bullet kill you without hurting you?

Her forward progress continued unchecked and she collided with Jason, taking them both to the floor. There was blood, she could feel it and smell it, but still she felt no pain.

Lying on top of Jason she became aware that he was not moving. She pushed herself off of him and checked herself for wounds. Finding none she looked at him and saw that he had been shot. She looked around the room wildly and saw Clint Adams coming in through the window.

"Oh, God," she cried out.

"Darcy? Are you all right?"

"Oh, God," she said again, sitting on the floor on her butt, naked and stained with Jason's blood.

"Darcy?" He hunched down next to her.

"It's not my blood," she said. "It's not my blood."

"Okay," he said, "you're okay."

He checked Lyle Jason and he was dead. Clint had fired the shot while hanging by a rope outside the window. It was the most off balance shot he had ever fired, and he had hit Jason right in the head.

Even he was impressed.

Epilogue

Clint, Cable, and Darcy were leaving Denver on the same day—two days after Lyle Jason and Earl Terry were killed—and went to the train station together.

"i guess you two will be getting back to your partnership, and your careers in the Service," Clint said.

"And what are you going back to?" Darcy asked.

"My life," he said.

"Traveling?" Darcy asked. "Butting into other people's business again?"

Clint spread his arms.

"Whatever comes along."

"You have no goals?" Cable asked.

"When you've lived your life the way I have," Clint said, "every day that you're still alive is a goal reached."

Their train was leaving a half hour before his, so he walked them to it.

"Thanks for your help," Cable said, shaking hands. He looked at Darcy and said, "I'll wait on the train."

When he was gone she looked at Clint.

"I don't know if it was worth it," she said. "Four agents died so I could catch my sister's killer."

"He wasn't just your sister's killer," Clint said. "He and Terry killed a lot of people, and they won't anymore."

"Thanks to you," she said. "Maybe if I hadn't been so driven by revenge someone else would have stopped them."

"Maybe," he said. "And maybe you've learned something about revenge that some people never learn."

"Will I see you again?"

"Who knows?" he said. "I come to Washington from time to time."

"Look me up."

She kissed him gently on the lips, and he helped her up onto the train.

"Hey," he said, "if you ever do meet Jim West, give him my best, huh?"

"I'll do that."

He watched as the train pulled out, then turned and walked toward his own train.

Watch for

WINNING STREAK

182nd novel in the exciting GUNSMITH series
from Jove

Coming in February!

J. R. ROBERTS

THE GUNSMITH